MY SISTER,
THE SERIAL KILLER

MY SISTER, THE
SERIAL KILLER

OYINKAN BRAITHWAITE

atlantic·*fiction*

First published in the United States in 2018 by Doubleday,
a division of Penguin Random House LLC.

First published in Great Britain in 2018 by Atlantic Books,
an imprint of Atlantic Books Ltd.

Originally published in Nigeria, in a different form, as an
ebook entitled *Thicker Than Water* by Qamina, Lagos, in 2017.

10 9 8 7 6 5 4 3 2

A CIP catalogue record for this book is available from the
British Library.

Hardback ISBN: 978 1 78649 597 6
Trade Paperback ISBN: 978 1 78649 762 8
E-book ISBN: 978 1 78649 599 0

Printed in Great Britain

Atlantic Books
An Imprint of Atlantic Books Ltd
Ormond House
26–27 Boswell Street
London
WC1N 3JZ

www.atlantic-books.co.uk

For my family, whom I love very much:

Akin, Tokunbo, Obafunke, Siji, Ore

MY SISTER,
THE SERIAL KILLER

WORDS

Ayoola summons me with these words—Korede, I killed him.

I had hoped I would never hear those words again.

BLEACH

I bet you didn't know that bleach masks the smell of blood. Most people use bleach indiscriminately, assuming it is a catchall product, never taking the time to read the list of ingredients on the back, never taking the time to return to the recently wiped surface to take a closer look. Bleach will disinfect, but it's not great for cleaning residue, so I use it only after I have first scrubbed the bathroom of all traces of life, and death.

It is clear that the room we are in has been remodeled recently. It has that never-been-used look, especially now that I've spent close to three hours cleaning up. The hardest part was getting to the blood that had seeped in between the shower and the caulking. It's an easy part to forget.

There's nothing placed on any of the surfaces; his shower gel, toothbrush and toothpaste are all stored in the cabinet above the sink. Then there's the shower mat—a black smiley face on a yellow rectangle in an otherwise white room.

Ayoola is perched on the toilet seat, her knees raised

and her arms wrapped around them. The blood on her dress has dried and there is no risk that it will drip on the white, now glossy floors. Her dreadlocks are piled atop her head, so they don't sweep the ground. She keeps looking up at me with her big brown eyes, afraid that I am angry, that I will soon get off my hands and knees to lecture her.

I am not angry. If I am anything, I am tired. The sweat from my brow drips onto the floor and I use the blue sponge to wipe it away.

I was about to eat when she called me. I had laid everything out on the tray in preparation—the fork was to the left of the plate, the knife to the right. I folded the napkin into the shape of a crown and placed it at the center of the plate. The movie was paused at the beginning credits and the oven timer had just rung, when my phone began to vibrate violently on my table.

By the time I get home, the food will be cold.

I stand up and rinse the gloves in the sink, but I don't remove them. Ayoola is looking at my reflection in the mirror.

"We need to move the body," I tell her.

"Are you angry at me?"

Perhaps a normal person would be angry, but what I feel now is a pressing need to dispose of the body. When I got here, we carried him to the boot of my car, so that I was free to scrub and mop without having to countenance his cold stare.

"Get your bag," I reply.

We return to the car and he is still in the boot, waiting for us.

The third mainland bridge gets little to no traffic at this time of night, and since there are no lamplights, it's almost pitch-black, but if you look beyond the bridge you can see the lights of the city. We take him to where we took the last one—over the bridge and into the water. At least he won't be lonely.

Some of the blood has seeped into the lining of the boot. Ayoola offers to clean it, out of guilt, but I take my homemade mixture of one spoon of ammonia to two cups of water from her and pour it over the stain. I don't know whether or not they have the tech for a thorough crime scene investigation in Lagos, but Ayoola could never clean up as efficiently as I can.

THE NOTEBOOK

"Who was he?"

"Femi."

I scribble the name down. We are in my bedroom. Ayoola is sitting cross-legged on my sofa, her head resting on the back of the cushion. While she took a bath, I set the dress she had been wearing on fire. Now she wears a rose-colored T-shirt and smells of baby powder.

"And his surname?"

She frowns, pressing her lips together, and then she shakes her head, as though trying to shake the name back into the forefront of her brain. It doesn't come. She shrugs. I should have taken his wallet.

I close the notebook. It is small, smaller than the palm of my hand. I watched a TEDx video once where the man said that carrying around a notebook and penning one happy moment each day had changed his life. That is why I bought the notebook. On the first page, I wrote, *I saw a white owl through my bedroom window*. The notebook has been mostly empty since.

"It's not my fault, you know." But I don't know. I don't know what she is referring to. Does she mean the inability to recall his surname? Or his death?

"Tell me what happened."

THE POEM

Femi wrote her a poem.

(She can remember the poem, but she cannot remember his last name.)

I dare you to find a flaw
in her beauty;
or to bring forth a woman
who can stand beside
her without wilting.

And he gave it to her written on a piece of paper, folded twice, reminiscent of our secondary school days, when kids would pass love notes to one another in the back row of classrooms. She was moved by all this (but then Ayoola is always moved by the worship of her merits) and so she agreed to be his woman.

On their one-month anniversary, she stabbed him in the bathroom of his apartment. She didn't mean to, of course. He was angry, screaming at her, his onion-stained breath hot against her face.

(But why was she carrying the knife?)

The knife was for her protection. You never knew with men, they wanted what they wanted when they wanted it. She didn't mean to kill him; she wanted to warn him off, but he wasn't scared of her weapon. He was over six feet tall and she must have looked like a doll to him, with her small frame, long eyelashes and rosy, full lips.

(Her description, not mine.)

She killed him on the first strike, a jab straight to the heart. But then she stabbed him twice more to be sure. He sank to the floor. She could hear her own breathing and nothing else.

BODY

Have you heard this one before? Two girls walk into a room. The room is in a flat. The flat is on the third floor. In the room is the dead body of an adult male. How do they get the body to the ground floor without being seen?

First, they gather supplies.

"How many bedsheets do we need?"

"How many does he have?" Ayoola ran out of the bathroom and returned armed with the information that there were five sheets in his laundry cupboard. I bit my lip. We needed a lot, but I was afraid his family might notice if the only sheet he had was the one laid on his bed. For the average male, this wouldn't be all that peculiar—but this man was meticulous. His bookshelf was arranged alphabetically by author. His bathroom was stocked with the full range of cleaning supplies; he even bought the same brand of disinfectant as I did. And his kitchen shone. Ayoola seemed out of place here—a blight in an otherwise pure existence.

"Bring three."

Second, they clean up the blood.

I soaked up the blood with a towel and wrung it out in

the sink. I repeated the motions until the floor was dry. Ayoola hovered, leaning on one foot and then the other. I ignored her impatience. It takes a whole lot longer to dispose of a body than to dispose of a soul, especially if you don't want to leave any evidence of foul play. But my eyes kept darting to the slumped corpse, propped up against the wall. I wouldn't be able to do a thorough job until his body was elsewhere.

Third, they turn him into a mummy.

We laid the sheets out on the now dry floor and she rolled him onto them. I didn't want to touch him. I could make out his sculpted body beneath his white tee. He looked like a man who could survive a couple of flesh wounds, but then so had Achilles and Caesar. It was a shame to think that death would whittle away at his broad shoulders and concave abs, until he was nothing more than bone. When I first walked in I had checked his pulse thrice, and then thrice more. He could have been sleeping, he looked so peaceful. His head was bent low, his back curved against the wall, his legs askew.

Ayoola huffed and puffed as she pushed his body onto the sheets. She wiped the sweat off her brow and left a trace of blood there. She tucked one side of a sheet over him, hiding him from view. Then I helped her roll him and wrap him firmly within the sheets. We stood and looked at him.

"What now?" she asked.

Fourth, they move the body.

We could have used the stairs, but I imagined us carrying what was clearly a crudely swaddled body and meeting someone on our way. I made up a couple of possible explanations—

"We are playing a prank on my brother. He is a deep sleeper and we are moving his sleeping body elsewhere."

"No, no, it's not a real man, what do you take us for? It's a mannequin."

"No, ma, it is just a sack of potatoes."

I pictured the eyes of my make-believe witness widening in fear as he or she ran to safety. No, the stairs were out of the question.

"We need to take the lift."

Ayoola opened her mouth to ask a question and then she shook her head and closed it again. She had done her bit, the rest she left to me. We lifted him. I should have used my knees and not my back. I felt something crack and dropped my end of the body with a thud. My sister rolled her eyes. I took his feet again, and we carried him to the doorway.

Ayoola darted to the lift, pressed the button, ran back to us and lifted Femi's shoulders once more. I peeked out of the apartment and confirmed that the landing was still clear. I was tempted to pray, to beg that no door be opened as we journeyed from door to lift, but I am fairly certain that those are exactly the types of prayers He *doesn't* answer. So I chose instead to rely on luck and speed. We silently shuffled across the stone floor. The lift dinged just in time and opened its mouth for us. We stayed to one side while I confirmed that the lift was empty, and then we heaved him in, bundling him into the corner, away from immediate view.

"Please hold the lift!" cried a voice. From the corner of my eye, I saw Ayoola about to press the button, the one that stops the lift from closing its doors. I slapped her hand away and jabbed the ground button repeatedly. As the lift doors slid shut, I caught a glimpse of a young mother's disappointed face. I felt a little guilty—she had a baby in one arm and bags in the other—but I did not feel guilty enough to risk incarceration. Besides, what good could she be up to moving around at that hour, with a child in tow?

"What is wrong with you?" I hissed at Ayoola, even though I knew her movement had been instinctive, possibly the same impulsiveness that caused her to drive knife into flesh.

"My bad," was her only response. I swallowed the words that threatened to spill out of my mouth. This was not the time.

On the ground floor, I left Ayoola to guard the body and hold the lift. If anyone was coming toward her, she was to shut the doors and go to the top floor. If someone attempted to call it from another floor, she was to hold the lift doors. I ran to get my car and drove it to the back door of the apartment building, where we fetched the body from the lift. My heart only stopped hammering in my chest when we shut the boot.

Fifth, they bleach.

SCRUBS

The administration at the hospital decided to change the nurses' uniform from white to pale pink, as the white was beginning to look more like curdled cream. But I stick with my white—it still looks brand-new.

Tade notices this.

"What's your secret?" he asks me as he touches the hem of my sleeve. It feels like he has touched my skin—heat flows through my body. I hand him the chart of the next patient and I try to think of ways to keep the conversation going, but the truth is, there is no way to make cleaning sound sexy—unless you are cleaning a sports car, in a bikini.

"Google is your friend," I say.

He laughs at me and looks down at the chart, then groans.

"Mrs. Rotinu, again?"

"I think she just likes seeing your face, Doctor." He looks up at me and grins. I try to smile back without betraying the fact that his attention has made my mouth go dry. As I exit the room, I swing my hips the way Ayoola is fond of doing.

"Are you okay?" he calls after me as my hand reaches the doorknob. I turn to face him.

"Hmmm?"

"You're walking funny."

"Oh, uh—I pulled a muscle." *Shame, I know thy name.* I open the door and leave the room quickly.

Mrs. Rotinu is seated on one of our many leather sofas in reception. She has one entirely to herself, and she has used the excess space to settle her handbag and makeup bag next to her. The patients look up as I head toward them, hoping it is now their turn. Mrs. Rotinu is powdering her face, but she pauses as I approach her.

"Is the doctor ready to see me now?" she asks. I nod and she stands, clicking the powder case shut. I gesture for her to follow, but she stops me with a hand on my shoulder: "I know the way."

Mrs. Rotinu has diabetes—type 2; in other words, if she eats right, loses some weight, and takes her insulin on time, there is no reason for us to see her as often as we do. And yet here she is, half skipping to Tade's office. I understand, though. He has the ability to look at you and make you feel like you are the only thing that matters for as long as you have his attention. He doesn't look away, his eyes don't glaze over, and he is generous with his smile.

I redirect my steps to the reception desk and slam my clipboard on it, hard enough to wake Yinka, who has found a way to sleep with her eyes open. Bunmi frowns at me because she is on the phone booking in a patient.

"What the hell, Korede? Don't wake me up unless there's a fire."

"This is a hospital, not a bed and breakfast."

She mutters "Bitch" as I walk away, but I ignore her. Something else has caught my attention. I let the air out through my teeth and go to find Mohammed. I sent him to the third floor an hour ago, and sure enough, he is still there, leaning on his mop and flirting with Assibi, she of the long, permed hair and startlingly thick eyelashes, another cleaner. She makes a run for it as soon as she sees me coming down the corridor. Mohammed turns to face me.

"Ma, I was just—"

"I don't care. Did you wipe the windows in reception with hot water and one-quarter distilled vinegar, like I asked you to?"

"Yes, ma."

"Okay . . . show me the vinegar." He shifts from foot to foot, staring at the floor and trying to figure out how to weave his way out of the lie he has just told. It comes as no surprise to me that he can't clean windows—I can smell him from ten feet away, and it is a rank, stale odor. Unfortunately, the way a person smells is not grounds for dismissal.

"I no see where I go buy am from."

I give him directions to the local store, and he slouches off to the staircase, leaving his bucket in the middle of the hallway. I summon him back to clean up after himself.

When I return to the ground floor, Yinka is asleep again—her eyes staring into nothing, much the way Femi's did. I blink the image from my mind and turn to Bunmi.

"Is Mrs. Rotinu done?"

"No," Bunmi replies. I sigh. There are other people in the waiting room. And all the doctors seem to be occupied with talkative people. If I had my way, each patient would have a fixed consultation time.

THE PATIENT

The patient in room 313 is Muhtar Yautai.

He is lying on the bed, his feet dangling over the end. He has daddy longlegs limbs, and the torso to which they are attached is quite long too. He was thin when he got here, but has gotten thinner still. If he does not wake soon, he will waste away.

I lift the chair from beside the table in the corner of the room and set it down a few inches from his bed. I sit on it, resting my head in my hands. I can feel a headache coming on. I came to talk to him about Ayoola, but it is Tade whom I cannot seem to get out of my mind.

"I . . . I wish . . ."

There is a comforting beep every few seconds from the machine monitoring his heart. Muhtar doesn't stir. He has been in this comatose state for five months—he was in a car accident with his brother, who was behind the wheel. All the brother got for his efforts was whiplash.

I met Muhtar's wife once; she reminded me of Ayoola. It wasn't that her looks were memorable, but she seemed completely oblivious to all but her own needs.

"Isn't it expensive to keep him in a coma like this?" she had asked me.

"Do you want to pull the plug?" I returned.

She raised her chin, offended by my question. "It is only proper that I know what I am getting myself into."

"I understood that the money was coming from his estate . . ."

"Well, yes . . . but . . . I . . . I'm just . . ."

"Hopefully, he will come out of the coma soon."

"Yes . . . hopefully."

But a lot of time has passed since that conversation and the day is drawing near when even his children will think shutting off his life support is best for everyone.

Until then, he plays the role of a great listener and a concerned friend.

"I wish Tade would see me, Muhtar. *Really* see me."

HEAT

The heat is oppressive, and so we find ourselves conserving our energy by restricting our movements. Ayoola is draped across my bed in her pink lace bra and black lace thong. She is incapable of practical underwear. Her leg is dangling off one end, her arm dangling off the other. Hers is the body of a music video vixen, a scarlet woman, a succubus. It belies her angelic face. She sighs occasionally to let me know she is alive.

I called the air conditioner repairman, who insisted he was ten minutes away. That was two hours ago.

"I'm dying here," Ayoola moans.

Our house girl ambles in carrying a fan and places it facing Ayoola, as though she is blind to the sweat rolling down my face. The loud whirring sound of the blades is followed by a gust of air, and the room cools very slightly. I lower my legs from the sofa and drag myself to the bathroom. I fill the basin with cold water and rinse my face, staring at the water as it ripples. I imagine a body floating away. What would Femi think of his fate, putrefying under the third mainland bridge?

At any rate, the bridge is no stranger to death.

Not long ago, a BRT bus, filled to the brim with passengers, drove off the bridge and into the lagoon. No one survived. Afterward, the bus drivers took to shouting, "Osa straight! Osa straight!" to their potential customers. Lagoon straight! Straight to the lagoon!

Ayoola lumbers in, pulling down her knickers: "I need to pee." She plops herself on the toilet seat and sighs happily as her urine pitter-patters into the ceramic bowl.

I pull the plug in the basin and walk out. It's too hot to protest the use of my facilities, or to point out that she has her own. It's too hot to speak.

I lie on my bed, taking advantage of Ayoola's absence, and close my eyes. And there he is. Femi. His face forever etched into my mind. I can't help but wonder what he was like. I met the others before they lost their lives, but Femi was a stranger to me.

I knew she was seeing someone, the signs were all there—her coy smiles, the late-night conversations. I should have paid closer attention. If I had met him, perhaps I would have seen this temper she claims he had. Perhaps I could have steered her away from him, and we would have been able to avoid this outcome.

I hear the toilet flush just as Ayoola's phone vibrates beside me, giving me an idea. Her phone is password protected, if you can call "1234" protection. I go through her many selfies until I find a picture of him. His mouth is set in a firm line, but his eyes are laughing. Ayoola is in the shot, looking lovely as usual, but his energy fills the screen. I smile back at him.

"What are you doing?"

"You got a message," I inform her, swiping quickly to return to the home page.

INSTAGRAM

#FemiDurandIsMissing has gone viral. One post in particular is drawing a lot of attention—Ayoola's. She has posted a picture of them together, announcing herself as the last person to have seen him alive, with a message begging anyone, *anyone,* to come forward if they know anything that can be of help.

She was in my bedroom when she posted this, just as she is now, but she didn't mention what she was up to. She says it makes her look heartless if she says nothing; after all, he was her boyfriend. Her phone rings and she picks it up.

"Hello?"

Moments later she kicks me.

"What the—?"

It's Femi's mother, she mouths. I feel faint; how the hell did she get Ayoola's number? She puts the phone on loudspeaker.

"... dear, did he tell you if he was going to go anywhere?"

I shake my head violently.

"No, ma. I left him pretty late," Ayoola replies.

"He was not at work the next day."

"Ummm . . . sometimes he used to jog at night, ma."

"I know, I told him, I told him all the time it was not safe." The woman on the line starts to cry. Her emotion is so strong that I start to cry too—I make no sound, but the tears I have no right to burn my nose, my cheeks, my lips. Ayoola starts crying too. Whenever I do, it sets her off. It always has. But I rarely cry, which is just as well. Her crying is loud and messy. Eventually, the sobs turn to hiccups and we are quiet. "Keep praying for my boy," the woman says hoarsely, before hanging up.

I turn on my sister. "What the hell is the matter with you?"

"What?"

"Do you not realize the gravity of what you have done? Are you enjoying this?" I grab a tissue and hand it to her, then take some for myself.

Her eyes go dark and she begins to twirl her dreadlocks.

"These days, you look at me like I'm a monster." Her voice is so low, I can barely hear her.

"I don't think you're—"

"This is victim shaming, you know . . ."

Victim? Is it mere coincidence that Ayoola has never had a mark on her, from any of these incidents with these men; not even a bruise? What does she want from me? What does she want me to say? I count the seconds;

if I wait too long to respond, it will be a response in itself, but I'm saved by my door creaking open. Mum wanders in, one hand pinned to her half-formed gèlè.

"Hold this for me."

I stand up and hold the part of the gèlè that is loose. She angles herself to face my standing mirror. Her miniature eyes take in her wide nose and fat lips, too big for her thin oval face. The red lipstick she has painted on further accentuates the size of her mouth. My looks are the spitting image of hers. We even share a beauty spot below the left eye; the irony is not lost on me. Ayoola's loveliness is a phenomenon that took my mother by surprise. She was so thankful that she forgot to keep trying for a boy.

"I'm going to Sope's daughter's wedding. The both of you should come. You might meet someone there."

"No, thank you," I reply stiffly.

Ayoola smiles and shakes her head. Mum frowns at the mirror.

"Korede, you know your sister will go if you do; don't you want her to marry?" As if Ayoola lives by anyone's rules but her own. I choose not to respond to my mother's illogical statement, nor acknowledge the fact that she is far more interested in Ayoola's marital fate than in mine. It is as though love is only for the beautiful.

After all, *she* didn't have love. What she had was a politician for a father and so she managed to bag herself a man who viewed their marriage as a means to an end.

The gèlè is done, a masterpiece atop my mother's small head. She cocks her head this way and that, and then frowns, unhappy with the way she looks in spite of the gèlè, the expensive jewelry and the expertly applied makeup.

Ayoola stands up and kisses her on the cheek. "Now, don't you look elegant?" she says. No sooner is it said than it becomes true—our mother swells with pride, raises her chin and sets her shoulders. She could pass for a dowager now at the very least. "Let me take a picture of you?" Ayoola asks, pulling out her phone.

Mum strikes what seems like a hundred poses, with Ayoola directing them, and then they scroll through their handiwork on the screen and select the picture that satisfies them—it is one of my mum in profile with her hand on her hip and her head thrown back in laughter. It is a nice picture. Ayoola busies herself on the phone, chewing on her lip.

"What are you doing?"

"Posting it on Instagram."

"Are you nuts? Or have you forgotten your previous post?"

"What's her previous post?" interjects Mum.

I feel a chill go through my body. It has been happening a lot lately. Ayoola answers her.

"I . . . Femi is missing."

"Femi? That fine boy you were dating?"

"Yes, Mum."

"Jésù ṣàànú fún wa! Why didn't you tell me?"

"I . . . I . . . was in shock."

Mum rushes over to Ayoola and pulls her into a tight embrace.

"I'm your mum, you must tell me everything. Do you understand?"

"Yes, ma."

But of course she can't. She can't tell her everything.

TRAFFIC

I am sitting in my car, fiddling with the knob, switching between channels because there is nothing else to do. Traffic plagues this city. It is only 5:15 a.m. and my car is one among many packed tightly on the road, unable to move. My foot is tired of tapping on and off the brake.

I look up from the radio and I inadvertently meet the eye of one of the LASTMA officials lurking around the line of cars, watching out for his next hapless victim. He sucks in his cheeks, frowns and walks toward me.

My heart drops to the floor, but there is no time to pick it back up. I tighten my fingers around the wheel to still the tremor in my hand. I know this has nothing to do with Femi. It can't have anything to do with Femi. Lagos police are not even half that efficient. The ones tasked with keeping our streets safe spend most of their time ferreting out money from the general public to bolster their meager salary. There is no way they could be on to us already.

Besides, this man is LASTMA. His greatest task, his raison d'être: to chase down individuals who run a red light. At least, this is what I tell myself as I begin to feel faint.

The man knocks on my window. I wind it down a few inches—enough to prevent angering him, but not enough for his hand to slip through and unlock my door.

He rests his hand on my roof and leans forward, as though we were two friends about to have a casual tête-à-tête. His yellow shirt and brown khakis are starched to an inch of their life, so much so that even the strong wind is unable to stir the fabric. An orderly uniform is a reflection of the owner's respect for his profession; at least, that's what it is supposed to mean. His eyes are dark, two wells in a vast desert—he is almost as light as Ayoola. He smells of menthol.

"Do you know why I have stopped you?"

I am tempted to point out that it is the traffic that has stopped me, but the futility of my position is all too clear. I have no way to escape.

"No, sir," I reply as sweetly as I can. Surely if they were on to us, it's not LASTMA that they would send, and they wouldn't do it here. Surely . . .

"Your seat belt. You are not wearing your seat belt."

"Oh . . ." I allow myself to breathe. The cars in front of me inch forward, but I am forced to stay in place.

"License and registration, please." I am loath to give this man my license. It would be as foolhardy as allowing him to enter my car—then he would call the shots. I don't answer immediately, so he tries to open my door, grunting when he finds it locked. He stands up straight, his conspiratorial manner flung away. "Madam, I said license and registration!" he barks.

On a normal day, I would fight him, but I cannot draw attention to myself right now, not while I'm driving the car that transported Femi to his final resting place. My mind wanders to the ammonia blemish in the boot.

"Oga," I say with as much deference as I can muster, "no vex. It was a mistake. E no go happen again." My words are more his than mine. Educated women anger men of his ilk, and so I try to adopt broken English, but I suspect my attempt betrays my upbringing even more.

"This woman, open the door!"

Around me cars continue to press forward. Some people give me a look of sympathy, but no one stops to help.

"Oga, please let's talk, I'm sure we can reach an understanding." My pride has divorced itself from me. But what can I do? Any other time, I would be able to call this man the criminal that he is, but Ayoola's actions have made me cautious. The man crosses his arms, dissatisfied but willing to listen. "I no go lie, I don't have plenty money. But if you go gree—"

"Did you hear me ask for money?" he asks, fiddling once again with my door handle, as though I'd be silly enough to unlock it. He straightens up and puts his hands on his hips. "Oya park!"

I open my mouth and shut it again. I just look at him.

"Unlock your car. Or we go tow am to the station and we go settle am there." My pulse is thumping in my ears. I can't risk them searching the car.

"Oga abeg, let's sort am between ourselves." My plea sounds shrill. He nods, glances around and leans forward again.

"Wetin you talk?"

I bring 3,000 naira out of my wallet, hoping it is enough and that he will accept it quickly. His eyes light up, but he frowns.

"You are not serious."

"Oga, how much you go take?"

He licks his lips, leaving a large dollop of spittle to glisten at me. "Do I look like a small pikin?"

"No, sir."

"So give me wetin a big man go use enjoy."

I sigh. My pride waves me goodbye as I add another 2,000 to the money. He takes it from me and nods solemnly.

"Wear your seat belt, and make you no do am again."

He wanders off, and I pull my seat belt on. Eventually, the tremors still.

RECEPTION

A man enters the hospital and makes a beeline for the reception desk. He is short, but he makes up for that in girth. He barrels toward us, and I brace myself for the impact.

"I have an appointment!"

Yinka grits her teeth and offers him her best smile. "Good morning, sir, can I take your name?"

He tosses her his name and she checks the files, thumbing through them slowly. You can't rush Yinka, but she slows down intentionally when you push her buttons. Soon the man is tapping his fingers, then his feet. She raises her eyes and peers at him through her lashes, then lowers them again and continues her search. He starts to puff up his cheeks; he is about to explode. I consider stepping in and diffusing the situation, but a yelling from a patient might do Yinka some good, so I settle back into my seat and watch.

My phone lights up and I glance at it. Ayoola. It is the third time she has called, but I am not in the mood to talk to her. Maybe she is reaching out because she has sent another man to his grave prematurely, or maybe she wants to know if I can buy eggs on the way home. Either way, I'm not picking up.

"Ah, here it is," Yinka cries, even though I have seen her examine that exact file twice and continue her search. He breathes out through his nostrils.

"Sir, you are thirty minutes late for your appointment."

"Ehen?"

It is her turn to breathe out.

This morning is quieter than usual. From where we sit, we can see everyone in the waiting area. It is shaped like an arc, with the reception desk and sofas facing the entrance and a large-screen TV. If we dimmed the lights, we would have ourselves a personal cinema. The sofas are a rich burgundy color, but everything else is devoid of color. (The decorator was not trying to broaden anyone's horizons.) If hospitals had a flag it would be white—the universal sign for surrender.

A child runs out of the playroom to her mum and then runs back in. There is no one else waiting to be attended to except the man who is right now getting on Yinka's nerves. She sweeps a curl of Monrovian hair from her eyes and stares at him.

"Have you eaten today, sir?"

"No."

"Okay, good. According to your chart, you haven't had a blood sugar test in a while. Would you like to have one?"

"Yes. Put it there. How much is it?" She tells him the price, and he hisses.

"You are very foolish. Abeg, what do I need that for? You people will just be calling price anyhow, as if you are paying someone's bill!"

Yinka glances my way. I know she is checking if I am still there, still watching her. She is recalling that if she steps out of line she will be forced to listen to my well-rehearsed speech about the code and culture of St. Peter's. She smiles through clenched teeth.

"No blood sugar test it is then, sir. Please take a seat, and I will let you know when the doctor is ready to see you."

"You mean he is not free now?"

"No. Unfortunately you are now"—she checks her watch—"forty minutes late, so you'll have to wait till the doctor has a free appointment."

The man gives a terse shake of his head and then takes his seat, staring at the television. After a minute he asks us to change the channel. Yinka mutters a series of curses under her breath, masked only by the occasional sounds of delight from the child in the sunny playroom and the football commentary from the TV.

DANCING

There is music blasting from Ayoola's room. She is listening to Whitney Houston's "I Wanna Dance with Somebody." It would be more appropriate to play Brymo or Lorde, something solemn or yearning, rather than the musical equivalent of a packet of M&MS.

I want to have a shower, to rinse the smell of the hospital's disinfectant off my skin, but instead I open the door. She doesn't sense my presence—she has her back to me and is thrusting her hips from side to side, her bare feet stroking the white fur rug as she steps this way and that. Her movements are in no way rhythmical; they are the movements of someone who has no audience and no self-consciousness to shackle them. Days ago, we gave a man to the sea, but here she is, dancing.

I lean on the door frame and watch her, trying and failing to understand how her mind works. She remains as impenetrable to me as the elaborate "artwork" daubed across her walls. She used to have an artist friend, who painted the bold black strokes over the whitewash. It feels out of place in this dainty room with its white furniture and plush toys. He would have been better off painting an angel or a fairy. At the time, I could tell that he hoped his generous act and his artistic talents would secure him a place in her heart, or at the very least a place in her bed, but he was short and had teeth that were fighting for space in his mouth. So all it got him was a pat on the head and a can of Coke.

She starts to sing; her voice is off-key. I clear my throat. "Ayoola."

She turns to me, still dancing; her smile spreads. "How was work?"

"It was alright."

"Cool." She shakes her hips and bends her knees. "I called you."

"I was busy."

"Wanted to come and take you out for lunch."

"Thanks, but I normally eat lunch at work."

"Okay o."

"Ayoola," I begin again, gently.

"Hmmm?"

"Maybe I should take the knife."

She slows her movements, until all she is doing is swaying side to side with the occasional swing of her arm. "What?"

"I said, maybe I should take the knife."

"Why?"

"Well . . . you don't need it."

She considers my words. It takes her the time it takes paper to burn.

"No thanks. I think I'll hold on to it." She increases the

tempo of her dance, whirling away from me. I decide to try a different approach. I pick up her iPod and turn the volume down. She faces me again and frowns. "What is it now?"

"It's not a good idea to have it, you know, in case the authorities ever come to the house to search. You could just toss it in the lagoon and reduce the risk of getting caught."

She crosses her arms and narrows her eyes. We stare at each other for a moment, then she sighs and drops her arms.

"The knife is important to me, Korede. It is all I have left of him."

Perhaps if it were someone else at the receiving end of this show of sentimentality, her words would hold some weight. But she cannot fool me. It is a mystery how much feeling Ayoola is even capable of.

I wonder where she keeps the knife. I never come across it, except in those moments when I am looking down at the bleeding body before me, and sometimes I don't even see it then. For some reason, I cannot imagine her resorting to stabbing if that particular knife were not in her hand; almost as if it were the knife and not her that was doing the killing. But then, is that so hard to believe? Who is to say that an object does not come with its own agenda? Or that the collective agenda of its previous owners does not direct its purpose still?

FATHER

Ayoola inherited the knife from him (and by "inherited" I mean she took it from his possessions before his body was cold in the ground). It made sense that she would take it—it was the thing he was most proud of.

He kept it sheathed and locked in a drawer, but he would bring it out whenever we had guests to show it off to. He would hold the nine-inch curved blade between his fingers, drawing the viewer's attention to the black comma-like markings carved and printed in the pale bone hilt. The presentation usually came with a story.

Sometimes, the knife was a gift from a university colleague—Tom, given to him for saving Tom's life during a boating accident. At other times, he had wrenched the knife from the hand of a soldier who had tried to kill him with it. Finally—and his personal favorite—the knife was in recognition of a deal he had made with a sheik. The deal was so successful that he was given the choice between the sheik's daughter and the last knife made by a long-dead craftsman. The daughter had a lazy eye, so he took the knife.

These stories were the closest things to bedtime tales we had. And we enjoyed the moment when he would bring out the knife with a flourish, his guests instinctively shrinking back. He always laughed, encouraging them to examine the weapon. As they oohed and aahed, he nodded, reveling in their admiration. Inevitably, someone would ask the question he was waiting for—"Where did you get it?"—and he would look at the knife as though seeing it for the first time, rotating it until it caught the light, before he launched into whichever tale he thought best for his audience.

When the guests were gone he would polish the knife meticulously with a rag and a small bottle of rotor oil, cleaning away the memory of the hands that had touched it. I used to watch as he squeezed a few drops of oil out, gently rubbing it along the blade with his finger in soft circular motions. This was the only time I ever witnessed tenderness from him. He took his time, rarely taking note of my presence. When he got up to rinse the oil from the blade, I would take my leave. It was by no means the end of the cleaning regimen, but it seemed best to be gone before it was over, in case his mood shifted during the process.

Once, when she thought he had gone out for the day, Ayoola entered his study and found his desk drawer unlocked. She took the knife out to look, smearing it with the chocolate she had just been eating. She was still in the room when he returned. He dragged her out by her hair, screaming. I turned up just in time to witness him fling her across the hallway.

I am not surprised she took the knife. If I had thought of it first, I would have taken a hammer to it.

KNIFE

Maybe she keeps it under her queen-sized bed or in her chest of drawers? Perhaps it is hidden in the pile of clothes stuffed into her walk-in closet? Her eyes follow mine as they roam the bedroom.

"You're not thinking of sneaking in here and taking it, are you?"

"I don't understand why you need it. It's dangerous to have it in the house. Give it to me, and I'll take care of it."

She sighs and shakes her head.

ÈFÓ

I took almost nothing from my father, in terms of looks. When I look at my mother, I am looking at my future self, though I could not be any less like her if I tried.

She is beached on the sofa in the downstairs living room, reading a Mills & Boon novel—a tale of the type of love she has never known. Beside her, in an armchair, Ayoola is hunched over, scrolling through her phone. I walk past them and reach for the adjoining door to the kitchen.

"You are going to cook?" my mum asks.

"Yes."

"Korede, teach your sister now. How will she look after her husband if she cannot cook?"

Ayoola pouts but says nothing. She doesn't mind being in the kitchen. She likes to sample everything she sets her eyes on.

In our home, the house girl and I do most of the cooking; my mother cooks too, but not as much as she used to when he was alive. Ayoola, on the other hand—well, it'll be interesting to see whether she can do anything more strenuous than putting bread in the toaster.

"Sure," I say, as Ayoola gets up to follow.

The house girl has prepared everything that I will need and set it aside on the counter, already washed and chopped. I like her. She is neat and has a calm demeanor, but more important, she knows nothing about him. We let go of all our staff after he passed, for "practical" reasons. We went a year with no help, which is harder than it sounds in a house of this size.

The chicken is already boiling. Ayoola opens the lid so the smell escapes, thick with fat and Maggi. "Mmm." She sucks in the aroma and moistens her cherry lips. The house girl blushes. "You try o!"

"Thank you, ma."

"Maybe I should help you taste if it is ready," Ayoola suggests, smiling.

"Maybe you could help by chopping the spinach."

Ayoola looks at all the prepped goods. "But it is already chopped na."

"I need more." The house girl hurries to get another bushel of spinach, but I call her back. "No, let Ayoola do it."

Ayoola sighs theatrically but fetches the spinach from the pantry. She picks up a knife, and unwittingly I think of Femi slumped in the bathroom, his hand not far from where the wound was, as though he had tried to stop the blood loss. How long was it before he died? Her grip is loose and the blade is pointed downward. She chops the spinach quickly and roughly, wielding the knife like a child would, with no care toward what the finished product will look like. I am tempted to stop her. The house girl tries not to laugh. I suspect that Ayoola is going out of her way to frustrate me.

I choose to ignore her and instead pour palm oil into a pot and add onions and peppers, which soon begin to fry.

"Ayoola, are you watching?"

"Mm-hmm," she replies as she leans on the counter and types furiously on her phone with one hand. She is still gripping the kitchen knife with the other. I go over to her, remove her fingers from the hilt and take the knife from her possession. She blinks.

"Please focus; after this we add the tàtàsé."

"Got it."

As soon as I turn my back, I hear the tapping sound of her keypad again. I am tempted to react, but I have left the palm oil for too long and it is beginning to spit and hiss at me. I reduce the heat of the flame and decide to forget about my sister for the time being. If she wants to learn, she will.

"What are we making again?"

Seriously?

"Ẹ̀fọ́," the house girl replies.

Ayoola nods solemnly and angles her phone over the pot of simmering ẹ̀fọ́, just as I add the spinach.

"Hey people, ẹ̀fọ́ loading!"

For a moment, I am frozen, spinach still in hand.

Could she really be uploading videos to Snapchat? Then I shake myself out of the trance. I grab the phone from her and hit delete, staining the screen with the oil on my hands.

"Hey!"

"Too soon, Ayoola. Way too soon."

#3

"Femi makes three, you know. Three, and they label you a serial killer."

I whisper the words in case anyone were to pass Muhtar's door. In case my words were to float through the two inches of wood and tickle the ears of a passerby. Aside from confiding in a comatose man, I take no risks. "Three," I repeat to myself.

Last night I couldn't sleep, so I stopped counting backward and sat at my desk, turning on my laptop. I found myself typing "serial killer" into the Google search box at 3 a.m. There it was: three or more murders . . . serial killer.

I rub my legs to rid them of the pins and needles that have set in. Is there any point in telling Ayoola what I have learned?

"Somewhere, deep down, she must know, right?"

I look at Muhtar. His beard has grown again. If it is not shaved at least once a fortnight, it gets knotted and threatens to cover half his face. Someone must have overlooked items in his care roster. Yinka is usually the culprit in matters such as these.

The faint sound of whistling in the corridor, drawing nearer. Tade. When he is not singing, he is humming, and when he tires of that, he whistles. He is a walking music box. The sound of him lifts my spirits. I walk to the door and open it just as he is approaching. He smiles at me.

I wave at him, then drop my hand, chastising myself for my eagerness. A smile would have been more than enough.

"I should have known you'd be here."

He opens the file he is carrying, glances at it and then hands it over. It is Muhtar's file. There is nothing of note in it. He hasn't gotten better or worse. The time when they will make the call is drawing nearer. I twist my head to get another look at Muhtar. He is at peace, and I envy him that. Every time I close my eyes I see a dead man. I wonder what it would be like to see nothing again.

"I know you care about him. I just want to make sure you're prepared if . . ." His voice trails off.

"He's a patient, Tade."

"I know, I know. But there's no shame in caring about another human being's fate."

He touches my shoulder gently, a gesture of comfort. Muhtar will die eventually, but he won't die in a pool of his own blood and he won't be devoured by the saltwater crabs that thrive in the water below the third mainland bridge. His family will know his fate. Tade's warm hand lingers on my shoulder, and I lean into it.

"On a more positive note, rumor has it you are going to be promoted to head nurse!" he tells me, abruptly removing his hand. It's not a huge surprise; the post has been vacant for some time and who else could fill it? Yinka? I'm much more concerned with the hand that no longer lingers on my shoulder.

"Great," I say, because that is what he'd expect me to say.

"When you get it, we will celebrate."

"Cool." I hope I sound nonchalant.

SONG

Tade has the smallest office of all the doctors, but I have never heard him complain. If it has even occurred to him that it may be unjust, he doesn't show it.

But today, the size of his office works to our advantage. At the sight of the needle, the little girl bolts for the door. Her legs are short, so she doesn't get far. Her mother grabs her.

"No!" cries the girl, kicking and scratching. She is like a wild chicken. Her mother grits her teeth and bears the pain. I wonder if this was what she imagined when she was posing for her pregnancy photo shoot and making merry at the baby shower.

Tade dips his hand into the bowl of candy he keeps on his desk for his child patients, but she smacks away the proffered lollipop. His smile does not falter; he begins to sing. His voice fills up the room, submerging my brain. Everything stills. The child pauses, confused. She looks up at her mother, who is transfixed by the voice too. It doesn't matter that he sings "Mary Had a Little Lamb." We still have goosebumps. Is there anything more beautiful than a man with a voice like an ocean?

I am standing beside the window, and I look down to see a group of people gathered, peering up and pointing. Tade rarely puts on the air conditioner and his window is usually open. He told me he likes to hear Lagos while he works—the never-ending car horns, the shouts of hawkers and tires screeching on the road. Now Lagos listens to him.

The little girl sniffs, and wipes away her mucus with the back of her hand. She waddles toward him. When she is older, she will remember him as her first love. She will think of how perfect his crooked nose was, and how soulful his eyes. But even if she forgets his face, his voice will stay with her in her dreams.

He scoops her into his arms and dries her tears with a tissue. He looks up at me expectantly and I shake myself out of my reverie. She doesn't notice as I approach her with the needle. She doesn't budge as I wipe her thigh with an alcohol swab. She tries to join him in song, her voice broken by the occasional sniff and hiccup. Her mother twists her wedding ring with her finger, as though contemplating taking it off. I consider passing her a tissue to catch the drool that threatens to spill from her mouth.

The little girl flinches as I inject the drug into her, but Tade's grip on her is firm. It's all over.

"Aren't you a brave girl?" he says to her. She beams

and this time is willing to collect her prize, a cherry-flavored lollipop.

"You are so good with kids," her mother coos. "Do you have any of your own?"

"No, I don't. One day, though." He smiles at her, showing off his perfect teeth and creasing his eyes. She can be forgiven for believing that this smile is just for her, but it is the smile he gives to everyone. It is the smile he gives to me. She blushes.

"And you are not married?" (Madam, do you want two husbands?)

"No, no, I'm not."

"I have a sister. She is very—"

"Dr. Otumu, here are the prescriptions."

Tade looks up at me, confused by my abruptness. Later, he will tell me gently, always gently, that I shouldn't cut patients off. They come to the hospital for healing and, sometimes, it's not just their bodies that need attention.

RED

Yinka is painting her nails at the reception desk. Bunmi sees me coming and nudges her, but it is a pointless warning—Yinka will not stop on my account. She acknowledges my presence with a feline smile.

"Korede, those shoes are nice o!"

"Thanks."

"The original must be very expensive."

Bunmi chokes on the water she is sipping, but I won't rise to the bait. Tade's voice is still ringing in my body, calming me as it calmed the child. I ignore her and turn to Bunmi.

"I'm going to take my lunch break now."

I head to the second floor with food in hand and knock on Tade's office door, waiting for his rich voice to grant entry. Gimpe, another cleaner (with all these cleaners, you would think the hospital would be spotless), looks my way and gives me a friendly, knowing smile—showing off her high cheekbones. I refuse to return it; she knows nothing about me. I try to bury my nerves and give the door another gentle knock.

"Come in."

I am not entering his office in my capacity as a nurse. My hands are holding a container of rice and ẹ̀fọ́. I can tell that the smell makes its way to him as soon as I walk in.

"To what do I owe this honor?"

"You rarely take advantage of your lunch break . . . so I thought I would bring lunch to you."

He accepts the container from me, and peers inside, inhaling deeply. "You made this? It smells exquisite!"

"Here." I hand him a fork and he digs in. He closes his eyes and sighs, and then opens them to smile at me.

"This is . . . Korede . . . men . . . you're going to make someone an awesome wife."

I'm sure the grin on my face is too big to be captured in a picture. I feel it all the way to my toes.

"I'm going to have to eat the rest of this later," he tells me, "I need to finish this report."

I stand up from the corner of the desk that I had made my temporary seat, and offer to stop by later for the Tupperware.

"Korede, seriously, thank you. You're the best."

There is a woman in the waiting room trying to calm a crying baby by rocking it back and forth, but the child won't be hushed. It is irritating some of the other patients who are waiting in reception. It is irritating me. I head toward her with a rattle, on the off chance that it will distract the baby, just as the entrance doors open—

Ayoola walks in, and every head turns her way and stays there. I stop where I am, rattle in hand, trying to understand what is happening. She looks as though she has brought the sunshine in with her. She is wearing a bright yellow shirtdress that by no means hides her generous breasts. Her feet are in green, strappy heels that make up for what she lacks in height, and she is holding a white clutch, big enough to house a nine-inch weapon.

She smiles at me, and saunters in my direction. I hear a man mutter "Damn" under his breath.

"Ayoola, what are you doing here?" My voice is tight in my throat.

"It's lunchtime!"

"And?"

She floats away not answering my question and heads toward the reception desk. Their eyes are fixed on her and she smiles her best smile. "You're my sister's friends?"

They open their mouths and shut them again.

"You're Korede's sister?" Yinka squeaks. I can see her trying to make the connection, measuring Ayoola's looks against mine. The resemblance is there—we share the same mouth, the same eyes—but Ayoola looks like a Bratz doll and I resemble a voodoo figurine. Yinka, who is arguably the most attractive employee at St. Peter's, with her cherub nose and wide lips, pales to the point of insignificance beside Ayoola. She knows it, too; she is twirling her expensive hair with her fingers and has pushed back her shoulders.

"What scent is that?" asks Bunmi. "It's like . . . it's really . . ."

Ayoola leans forward and whispers something into Bunmi's ear, and then she straightens up. "It's our little secret, okay?" She winks at Bunmi, and Bunmi's usually impassive face lights up. I've had enough. I head toward the desk.

Just then, I hear Tade's voice and my heart quickens. I grab Ayoola, dragging her toward the exit.

"Hey!"

"You have to go!"

"What? Why? Why are you being so—"

"What's going . . ." Tade's voice trails to nothing and the blood cools within my body. Ayoola frees herself from my grip, but it doesn't matter; it's too late anyway. His eyes settle on Ayoola and dilate. He adjusts his coat. "What's going on?" he says again, his voice suddenly husky.

"I'm Korede's sister," she announces.

He looks from her to me, then back to her again. "I didn't know you had a sister?" He is talking to me, but his eyes have not left hers.

Ayoola pouts. "I think she is ashamed of me."

He smiles at her; it is a kind smile. "Of course not. Who could be? Sorry, I didn't get your name."

"Ayoola." She puts out her hand, the way a queen would for her subjects.

He takes it and gives it a gentle squeeze. "I'm Tade."

SCHOOL

I can't pinpoint the exact moment I realized that Ayoola was beautiful and I was . . . not. But what I do know is that I was aware of my own inadequacies long before.

Secondary school can be cruel. The boys would write lists of those who had a figure eight—like a Coca-Cola bottle—and those who had a figure one—like a stick. They would draw pictures of girls and exaggerate their best or worst features and tack them on the school notice board for the world to see—at least until the teachers took the pictures down, tearing them from the pins, an act that left a little shred of paper stuck like a taunt.

When they drew me, it was with lips that could belong to a gorilla and eyes that seemed to push every other feature out of the way. I told myself boys were immature and dumb, so it didn't matter that they didn't want me; and it didn't matter that some of them tried anyway because they assumed I'd be so grateful for the attention that I'd do whatever they wanted. I stayed away from all of them. I mocked girls for swooning over guys, judged them for kissing, and held them in contempt at every opportunity. I was above it all.

I was fooling no one.

Two years in, I was hardened and ready to protect my sister, who I was sure would receive the same treatment that I had. Maybe hers would be even worse. She would come to me each day weeping and I would wrap my arms around her and soothe her. It would be us against the world.

Rumor has it that she was asked out on her first day, by a boy in SS2. It was unprecedented. Boys in the senior classes didn't notice juniors, and when they did, they rarely tried to make it official. She said no. But I received the message loud and clear.

STAIN

"I just thought we should spend lunchtime together."

"No, you wanted to see where I work."

"And what's wrong with that, Korede?" my mother exclaims. "You've been working there for a year and your sister has never seen the place!" She is horrified by this, as she is by every injustice that she feels Ayoola suffers.

The house girl brings the stew out of the kitchen and sets it on the table. Ayoola leans forward and serves herself a bowlful. She has unwrapped the àmàlà and dipped it in the soup before my mother and I have finished serving ourselves.

We sit in our customary places at our rectangular table: my mother and I are seated on the left, Ayoola on the right. There used to be a chair at the head of the table, but I burnt it down to a crisp in a bonfire just outside our compound. We don't talk about that. We don't talk about him.

"Your aunty Taiwo called today," Mum begins.

"Did she now?"

"Yes. She says she would like to hear from both of you

more." Mum pauses, waiting for some sort of response from one of us.

"Can you pass the okro, please?" I ask.

My mother passes the okro.

"So," she pivots, seeing as her previous topic baited no one, "Ayoola said there is a cute doctor at your work."

I drop the bowl of okro and it spills on the table—it is green and filmy, quickly seeping into the floral tablecloth.

"Korede!"

I dab at it with a cloth but I can barely hear her—my thoughts are eating my brain.

I can feel Ayoola's eyes on me and I try to calm down. The house girl runs to clean the stain, but the water she uses makes the stain bigger than it was before.

HOME

I am staring at the painting that hangs above the piano nobody plays.

He commissioned it after he passed off a shipment of refurbished cars to a car dealership as brand-new—a painting of the house his dodgy deals had built. (Why have a painting of the house you live in, hanging inside said house?)

As a child I would go stand before it and wish myself inside. I imagined that our alternates were living within its watercolor walls. I dreamt that laughter and love lay beyond the green lawn, inside the white columns and the heavy oak door.

The painter even added a dog barking at a tree, as if he knew that we used to have one. She was soft and brown and she made the mistake of peeing in his office. We never saw her again. The painter could not have known this; and yet, there is a dog in the painting and sometimes I swear I could hear her bark.

The beauty of our home could never compare to the beauty of the painting, with its perpetual pink dawn and leaves that never withered, and its bushes, tinted with otherworldly shades of yellow and purple, ringing the garden. In the painting, the outside walls are always a crisp white, while in reality we have not been able to repaint them and they are now a bleached-out yellow.

When he died, I sold every other painting he had bought for the cash. It was no great loss. If I could have gotten rid of the house itself, I would have. But he had built our southern-style home from scratch, which meant no rent and no mortgage (besides, no one was interested in acquiring a home of that size, when the paperwork for the land it was built on was dubious at best). So instead of moving into a smaller apartment, we managed the maintenance costs of our grand, history-rich home as best we could.

I glance at the painting once more as I make the trip from bedroom to kitchen. There are no people in it, which is just as well. But if you squint, you can see a shadow through one of the windows that looks like it might be a woman.

"Your sister just wants to be around you, you know. You are her best friend." It is my mother. She comes to stand beside me. Mother still talks about Ayoola as if she were a child, rather than a woman who rarely hears the word "no." "What harm will it do if she comes to your workplace now and again?"

"It's a hospital, Mum, not a park."

"Eh, we have heard. You stare at that painting too much," she says, changing the subject. I look away, and instead direct my eyes to the piano.

We should really have sold the piano, too. I swipe my finger across the lid, making a line in the dust. My mother sighs and walks away, because she knows I won't be able to rest until there is not a speck of dust left on the piano's surface. I head to the supply cabinet and grab a set of wipes. If only I could wipe away all our memories with it.

BREAK

"You didn't tell me you have a sister."

"Mm."

"I mean, I know the school you went to and the name of your first boyfriend. I even know that you love to eat popcorn with syrup drizzled on it—"

"You really need to try it sometime."

"—but I didn't know you have a sister."

"Well, you know now."

I turn away from Tade and dispose of the needles on the metal tray. He could do it himself, but I like to find ways to make his work easier. He is hunched over his desk, scribbling on the page before him. No matter how quickly he writes, his handwriting is large and its loops connect letter to letter. It is neat and clear. The scratching sound of the pen stills, and he clears his throat.

"Is she seeing anyone?"

I think of Femi sleeping on the ocean bed, being nibbled at by fishes. "She is taking a break."

"A break?"

"Yes. She isn't going to be dating anyone for a while."

"Why?"

"Her relationships tend to end badly."

"Oh . . . guys can be jerks." This sounds strange coming from a guy, but Tade has always been sensitive. "Do you think she would mind if you gave me her number?" I think of Tade, fish swimming by as he drifts down toward the ocean bed, toward Femi.

I place the syringe back on the tray carefully so I don't accidentally stab myself with it.

"I'll have to ask her," I tell him, though I don't intend to ask Ayoola anything. If he doesn't see her, she will fade into the far reaches of his mind like a cold draft on an otherwise warm day.

FLAW

"So, you people share the same father and mother?"

"She told you she is my sister."

"But is she your full sister? She looks kinda mixed."

Yinka is really starting to piss me off. The sad thing is that her questions are neither the most obnoxious I have received in my lifetime nor the most uncommon. After all, Ayoola is short—her only flaw, if you consider that to be a flaw—whereas I am almost six feet tall; Ayoola's skin is a color that sits comfortably between cream and caramel and I am the color of a Brazil nut, before it is peeled; she is made wholly of curves and I am composed only of hard edges.

"Have you informed Dr. Imo that the X-ray is ready?" I snap.

"No, I—"

"Then I suggest you do that."

I walk away from her before she has a chance to finish her excuse. Assibi is making the beds on the second floor and Mohammed is flirting with Gimpe right in front of me. They're standing close to each other, his hand pressed on the wall as he leans toward her. He will have to wipe that spot down. Neither of them see me—his back is to me, and her eyes are cast down, lapping up the honeyed compliments he must be paying her. Can't she smell him? Perhaps she can't; Gimpe also gives off a rank smell. It is the smell of sweat, of unwashed hair, of cleaning products, of decomposed bodies under a bridge . . .

"Nurse Korede!"

I blink. The couple has vanished. Apparently I've been standing in the shadows for a while, lost in thought. Bunmi is looking at me quizzically. I wonder how many times she has called me. She is hard to read. There doesn't seem to be a whole lot going on in her frontal lobe.

"What is it?"

"Your sister is downstairs."

"Excuse me?"

I don't wait for her to repeat her statement and I don't wait for the lift—I run down the stairs. But when I get to the reception area, Ayoola is nowhere to be seen and I am panting for breath. Perhaps my colleagues have sensed how much my sister's presence here rattles me; maybe they are messing with me.

"Yinka, where is my sister?" I wheeze.

"Ayoola?"

"Yes. The only sister I have."

"How would I know? I didn't even know you had one sister before, for all I know you people are ten."

"Okay, fine, where is she?"

"She is in Dr. Otumu's office."

I take the stairs, two at a time. Tade's office is directly opposite the lift, so that every time I arrive on the second floor, I am tempted to knock on his door. Ayoola's laughter vibrates in the hallway—she has a big laugh, deep and unrestrained, the laughter of a person without a care in the world. On this occasion, I don't bother to knock.

"Oh! Korede, hi. I am sorry I stole your sister. I understand you two have a lunch date." I take in the scene. He has chosen not to sit behind his desk, but instead is sitting in one of the two chairs in front. Ayoola is perched on the other. Tade has angled his own seat so that it is facing her, and as though that were not enough, he leans forward, resting his elbows on his knees.

The top Ayoola has chosen to wear today is white and backless. Her leggings are a bright pink and her dreadlocks are piled atop her head. They look heavy, too heavy for her to bear, but her frame is straight. In her hands is his phone, where she was undoubtedly in the process of saving her number.

They look at me without a shadow of guilt.

"Ayoola, I told you I can't do lunch."

Tade is surprised by my tone. He frowns but says nothing. He is too polite to interrupt a squabble between sisters.

"Oh, that's okay. I spoke to that nice girl Yinka and she said she will cover for you." Oh, she would, would she?

"She shouldn't have done that. I have a lot of work to do."

Ayoola pouts. Tade clears his throat.

"You know, I haven't had *my* lunch break yet. If you're interested, I know a cool place around the corner."

He is talking about Saratobi. They serve a mean steak dish there. I took him there the day after I discovered it. Yinka tagged along, but even that could not ruin the lunch for me. I learned that Tade is an Arsenal supporter and he once tried his hand at professional football. I learned he is an only child. I learned he isn't a huge fan of vegetables. I had hoped one day we might repeat the experience—without Yinka—and I would learn more about him.

Ayoola beams at him.

"That sounds great. I hate to eat alone."

FLAPPER

When I burst into Ayoola's room that evening, she is sitting at her desk sketching a new design for her clothing line. She models the clothes she designs on social media, and can barely handle the number of orders that comes in. It is a marketing ploy: you look at a beautiful person with a great body and think maybe—if you combine the right clothes and accessorize appropriately— you can look as good as they do.

Her dreadlocks shield her face, but I don't need to see her to know she is chewing her lip and her eyebrows are furrowed in concentration. Her table is bare except for her sketchbook, pens and three bottles of water, one of which is almost empty. But everything else is upside down—her clothes are on the floor, spilling out of cupboards, and piled on her bed.

I pick up the shirt at my feet and fold it.

"Ayoola."

"What's up?" She doesn't look around or lift her head. I pick up another item of clothing.

"I would like it if you stopped coming to my place of work." I have gotten her attention now; she puts her pencil down and spins to face me, the locks spinning with her.

"Why?"

"I would just like to separate my work and home lives."

"Fine." She shrugs and turns back to the design. From where I stand I can see that it is a dress in the style of a twenties flapper.

"And I'd like you to stop talking to Tade."

She spins my way again, cocking her head to one side and frowning. It is odd to see her frown, she does it so rarely.

"Why?"

"I just don't think it is wise to start something with him."

"'Cause I'll hurt him?"

"I'm not saying that."

She pauses, considering my words.

"Do you like him?"

"That's really not the point. I don't think you should be seeing *anyone* right now."

"I told you I had to do it. I told you."

"I think you should just take a little break."

"If you want him for yourself, just say so." She pauses, giving me time to stake my claim. "Besides, he isn't all that different from the rest of them, you know."

"What are you talking about?" He *is* different. He is kind and sensitive. He sings to children.

"He isn't deep. All he wants is a pretty face. That's all they ever want."

"You don't know him!" My voice is higher than I expect it to be. "He is kind and sensitive and he—"

"Do you want me to prove it to you?"

"I just want you to stop talking to him, okay?"

"Well, we don't always get what we want." She swivels her chair, and continues her work. I should walk out, but instead I pick up the rest of her clothes and fold them one by one, clamping down on my anger and self-pity.

MASCARA

My hand isn't steady. You need steady hands when you are applying makeup, but I am not used to it. There never seemed to be much point in masking my imper- fections. It's as futile as using air freshener when you leave the toilet—it just inevitably ends up smelling like perfumed shit.

A YouTube video is streaming on the laptop beside me and I try to copy in my dressing-table mirror what the girl is doing, but our actions don't seem to be cor- responding. Still I persevere. I pick up the mascara and brush my lashes. They clump together. I try to sepa- rate them and end up inking my fingers. When I blink, traces of black gunk are left on the foundation around my eyes. It took me a while to do the foundation and I don't want it to smudge, so I just add more.

I examine my handiwork in the mirror. I look differ- ent, but whether I look better . . . I don't know. I look different.

The things that will go into my handbag are laid out on my dressing table.

Two packets of pocket tissue, one 30-centiliter bottle

of water, one first aid kit, one packet of wipes, one wallet, one tube of hand cream, one lip balm, one phone, one tampon, one rape whistle.

Basically, the essentials for every woman. I arrange the items in my shoulder bag and walk out of my bedroom, carefully shutting the door behind me. My mother and sister are still asleep, but I can hear the skittish movements of the house girl in the kitchen. I head down to meet her and she gives me my usual glass of orange, lime, pineapple and ginger juice. There is nothing like fruit juice to wake up your body.

When the clock strikes 5, I leave the house and negotiate the early-morning rush. I am at the hospital by 5:30. It is so quiet at this time of day that one is tempted to speak in whispers. I drop my bag behind the reception desk and pull down the incident book from the shelf to see if anything worthy of note took place during the night. One of the doors behind me squeaks open and soon Chichi is by my side.

It is the end of Chichi's shift, but she lingers. "Ah ah, are you wearing makeup?"

"Yes."

"What's the occasion?"

"I just decided to—"

"Wonders will never end, you even put plenty foundation!"

I resist the urge to grab the wipes out of my bag and remove every trace of makeup from my face right then and there.

"Abi, have you found boyfriend?"

"What?"

"You can tell me, I'm your friend." I can't tell her. Chichi will spread the news before I have finished telling it. And we are not friends. She smiles, hoping to put me at ease, but the expression does not sit comfortably on her face. Her forehead and cheeks are caked in a too-light concealer to hide her aggressive pimples (though she left puberty behind long before I was born), and her bright red lipstick has seeped into the cracks in her lips. I would be more at ease if the Joker were to smile at me.

Tade arrives at 9 a.m. He hasn't slipped on his doctor's coat yet and I can make out the muscles beneath his shirt. I try not to stare at them. I try not to dwell on the fact that they remind me of Femi's. The first thing he asks is, "How is Ayoola?" He used to ask how *I* was. I tell him she is fine. He peers at my face curiously.

"I didn't know you wore makeup."

"I don't really, I just thought I'd try something different . . . What do you think?"

He frowns as he considers my handiwork.

"I think I prefer you without it. You have nice skin, you know. Really smooth."

He has noticed my skin . . . !

At the first opportunity, I sidle off to the toilet to remove the makeup, but freeze when I see Yinka pursing her lips at one of the mirrors over the bank of sinks. I take a couple of silent steps backward, but she turns her head in my direction and raises her eyebrow.

"What are you doing?"

"Nothing. I'm leaving."

"But you just came in . . ."

She narrows her eyes, instantly suspicious, as she draws closer to me. The moment she realizes I have makeup on, she sneers.

"My, my, how the 'au natural' have fallen."

"It was just an experiment."

"An experiment in the winning of Dr. Tade's heart?"

"No! Of course not!"

"I'm playing with you. We both know Ayoola and Tade are meant to be. They look gorgeous together."

"Yes. Exactly."

Yinka smiles at me, but her smile is mocking. She sweeps past me as she leaves the toilet and I let go of the breath I've been holding. I rush to the sink and take a wipe from my bag, rubbing at my skin. When I've got the worst of it off, I splash my face with handfuls of water, rinsing away any traces of makeup and tears.

ORCHIDS

A bouquet of violently bright orchids is delivered to our house. For Ayoola. She leans forward and picks out the card that is tucked between the stems. She smiles.

"It is from Tade."

Is this how he sees her? As an exotic beauty? I console myself with the knowledge that even the most beautiful flowers wither and die.

She takes out her phone and begins to type a message, narrating her text out loud—"I. Really. Prefer. Roses." I should stop her, I really should. Tade is a man who puts a lot of thought into everything he does. I can see him in a flower shop, examining bouquet after bouquet, asking questions about varietals and feeding needs, making a well-informed choice. I select a vase from our collection and place the flowers on our center table. The walls are a solemn cream and the flowers light up the living room. "Send."

He will be taken aback by her text, disappointed and hurt. But perhaps he will understand that she is not the one for him and he will finally back off.

At noon, a spectacular bouquet of roses arrives at

our house, a mixture of red and white. Ayoola is out textile shopping, so the house girl hands them to me, despite us both knowing who they are for. They are not the already wilting roses with which Ayoola's admirers usually grace our table—these flowers are bursting with life. I try not to inhale the sickly sweet smell and I try not to cry.

Mum walks into the room and zeroes in on the flowers.

"Who are these from?"

"Tade," I hear myself say, even though Ayoola is not there and I have not opened the signature card.

"The doctor?"

"Yes."

"But didn't he already send orchids this morning?"

I sigh. "Yes. And now he's sent roses."

She breaks into a dreamy smile—she is already picking the aṣọ ẹbí and compiling the guest list for the wedding. I leave her there with the flowers and her fantasies and retire to my room. My bedroom has never seemed as devoid of life as it does now.

When Ayoola returns that evening, she fingers the roses, takes their picture and is about to post it online when I remind her, once again, that she has a boyfriend who has been missing for a month and whom she is supposed to be mourning. She pouts.

"How long am I meant to post boring, sad stuff?"

"You don't have to post at all."

"How long, though?"

"A year, I guess."

"You must be kidding me."

"Any shorter than that and you will, at the very least, look like a sorry excuse for a human being." She examines me to see if I already believe she is a sorry excuse for a human being. These days I don't know what or even how to think. Femi haunts me; he intrudes upon my thoughts uninvited. He forces me to doubt what I thought I understood. I wish he would leave me alone, but his words—his way of expressing himself—and his beauty set him apart from the others. And then there is her behavior. The last two times, at least she shed a tear.

ROSES

I can't sleep. I lie in bed, turning from back to side, from side to front. I switch the air conditioner on and off. Finally, I get out of bed and leave my room. The house is silent. Even the house girl is asleep. I head to the living room, where the flowers seem to be defying the darkness. I go to the roses first and touch the petals. I peel one off. Then another. Then another after that. Time passes slowly as I stand there in my nightie plucking flower after flower, till the petals are all scattered at my feet.

In the morning, I hear my mum shrieking—it invades my dream, pulling me back to consciousness. I fling back the blanket and dash out onto the landing; the door to Ayoola's room opens and I hear her behind me as we thunder downstairs. I feel a headache coming on. Last night, I tore apart two gorgeous bouquets of flowers and now my mother stands before their ruins, convinced that someone broke into the house.

The house girl runs into the room. "The front door is still locked, ma," she whines to my mother.

"Then . . . who could it . . . was it *you*?" Mum barks at the girl.

"No, ma. I wouldn't do that, ma."

"Then how did this happen?"

If I don't say something soon, my mum will decide it was the house girl and she will fire her. After all, who else could it have been? I bite my lip as my mother rails at the cowering girl, whose beaded cornrows quiver with her frame. She doesn't deserve the rebuke she is getting and I know I must speak up. But how will I explain the feeling that struck me? Must I confess to my jealousy?

"I did it."

They are Ayoola's words, not mine.

My mum stops mid-rant. "But . . . why would you . . ."

"We fought, last night. Tade and I. He dared me. So I pulled them apart. I should have thrown them away. I'm sorry."

She knows. Ayoola knows I did it. I keep my head down, looking at the petals on the floor. Why did I leave them there? I abhor untidiness. My mother shakes her head, trying to understand.

"I hope you . . . apologized to him."

"Yes, we have made up."

The house girl goes to get a broom to sweep away the remnants of my anger.

Ayoola and I don't discuss what has taken place.

FATHER

One day he was towering over me, spitting pure hell.
He reached for his cane and then he . . . slumped, hit-
ting his head against the glass coffee table as he fell to
the floor. His blood was brighter than the dark color we
saw on TV. I got up warily and Ayoola came out from
behind the couch, where she'd been taking cover. We
stood over him. For the first time, we were taller. We
watched the life seep out of him. Eventually, I woke my
mother up from her Ambien-induced sleep and told
her it was over.

It has been ten years now and we are expected to celebrate him, to throw an anniversary party in honor
of his life. If we do not we will end up fielding difficult
questions, and we are nothing if not thorough in our
deception of others.

"We could have something in the house?" Mum suggests to the awkward planning committee gathered in
the living room.

Aunty Taiwo shakes her head. "No, too small. My
brother deserves a grand celebration."

I am sure they are celebrating him in hell. Ayoola rolls her eyes and chews her gum, adding nothing to the conversation. Every once in a while, Aunty Taiwo sends a worried glance her way.

"Where do you want to do it, aunty?" I ask with icy politeness.

"There is a venue in Lekki that's really nice." She names the place, and I suck in my breath. The amount she has offered to contribute wouldn't even cover half the cost of a venue like that. She expects, of course, that we will dip into the funds he left and she can flex, show off to her friends and drink lots of champagne. He doesn't deserve a single naira, but my mother wants to keep up appearances and so she agrees. With the negotiations over with, Aunty Taiwo leans back against the sofa and smiles at us. "So are the two of you seeing anyone?"

"Ayoola is dating a doctor!" Mum announces.

"Ah, wonderful. You people are getting old o and the competition is tight. Girls are not joking. Some of them are even taking men away from their wives!" Aunty Taiwo is one such woman—married to a former governor who was already married when she met him. She is a curious woman, visiting us whenever she flies over from Dubai, seemingly impervious to our dislike of her. She never had any children and she has told us, time without number, that she considers us her surrogate daughters. We consider ourselves no such thing.

"Help me tell them o. It's like they just want to stay in this house forever."

"You know, men are very fickle. Give them what they want and they will do anything for you. Keep your hair long and glossy or invest in good weaves; cook for him and send the food to his home and his office. Stroke his ego in front of his friends and treat them well for his sake. Kneel down for his parents and call them on important days. Do these things and he will put a ring on your finger, fast fast."

My mother nods sagely. "Very good advice."

Of course, neither of us is listening. Ayoola has never needed help in the men department, and I know better than to take life directions from someone without a moral compass.

BRACELET

Tade comes to pick her up, Friday at seven. He is on time, but, of course, Ayoola is not. In fact, she has not even showered yet—she is stretched out on her bed laughing at videos of auto-tuned cats.

"Tade is here."

"He is early."

"It's past seven."

"Oh!"

But she doesn't move an inch. I go back downstairs to tell Tade she is getting ready.

"No problem, there's no rush."

My mum is sitting opposite him, beaming from ear to ear, and I join her on the sofa.

"You were saying?"

"Yes, I am passionate about real estate. My cousin and I are building a block of flats in Ibeju-Lekki. It'll take another three months or so to conclude the construction, but we already have takers for five of the flats!"

"That's amazing!" she cries, as she calculates his worth. "Korede, offer our guest something."

[❉]

"What would you like? Cake? Biscuits? Wine? Tea?"

"I wouldn't want to put you out of your way . . ."

"Just bring everything, Korede." So I get up and go to the kitchen, where the house girl is watching *Tinsel*. She jumps up when she sees me and assists in ransacking the larder. When I return with the goodies, Ayoola still has not appeared.

"This is delicious," Tade exclaims after taking his first bite of the cake. "Who made this?"

"Ayoola," my mum says quickly, shooting me a warning look. It is a stupid lie. It is a pineapple upside-down cake, sweet and soft, and Ayoola couldn't fry an egg to save her life. She rarely enters the kitchen, except to forage for snacks or under duress.

"Wow," he says, chewing happily. He is delighted by the news.

I see her first because I am facing the stairs. He follows my eyeline and twists his body around to see. I hear him suck in his breath. Ayoola is paused there, allowing herself to be admired. She is wearing the flapper dress she was sketching a few weeks ago. The gold beads blend wonderfully with her skin. Her dreads have been plaited into one long braid draped over her right shoulder and her heels are so high, a lesser woman would have already fallen down the stairs.

Tade stands up slowly and walks to meet her at the foot of the staircase. He brings out a long velvet box from his inner suit pocket.

"You look beautiful . . . This is for you."

Ayoola takes the gift and opens it. She smiles, lifting the gold bracelet so Mum and I can see.

TIME

#FemiDurandIsMissing has been sidelined by #NaijaJollofvsKenyanJollof. People may be drawn to the macabre, but never for very long, and so news of Femi's disappearance has been trumped by conversations about which country's jollof rice is better. Besides, he was almost thirty, not a child. I read the comments. Some people say he probably got fed up and left Lagos. Some suggest that perhaps he killed himself.

In an effort to keep people caring about Femi, his sister has started posting poetry from his blog—www.wildthoughts.com. I can't help but read them. He was very talented.

I found the quiet
In your arms;
The nothing that I search for
Daily.
You are empty
And I am full.
Fully drowning.

I wonder if this poem was about her. If he knew—

"What are you looking at?"

I slam the lid of my laptop closed. Ayoola is framed in the doorway of my bedroom. I narrow my eyes at her.

"Tell me what happened with Femi again," I ask her.

"Why?"

"Just humor me."

"I don't want to talk about it. It's upsetting to think about."

"You said he was aggressive toward you."

"Yes."

"As in, he grabbed you?"

"Yes."

"And you tried to run?"

"Yes."

"But . . . there was a stab wound in his back."

She sighs. "Look, I was afraid and then I kinda saw red. I don't know."

"Why were you afraid?"

"He was threatening me, threatening to, like, hit me and stuff. He had me cornered."

"But why? Why was he so angry?"

"I don't . . . I don't remember. I think he saw some messages from a guy on my phone or something and he just flipped."

"So he cornered you, how did you get to the knife? It was in your bag, wasn't it?"

She pauses. "I . . . I don't know . . . it was all a blur. I'd take it back if I could. I'd take it all back."

THE PATIENT

"I want to believe her. I want to believe it was self-defense . . . I mean the first time, I was furious. I was convinced Somto deserved it. And he had been so . . . slimy—always licking his lips, always touching her. I caught him scratching himself down there once, you know."

Muhtar doesn't stir. I imagine he tells me that scratching your balls is not a crime.

"No, of course not. But it's in character, I mean his whole . . . just sliminess and overall dirtiness made it easy to believe the things she accused him of. Even Peter was . . . dodgy. Said he did 'business' and always answered your questions with one of his own." I lean back, and close my eyes. "Everyone hates that. But Femi . . . he was different . . ."

Muhtar wonders how different he could have been. After all, it sounds as if he was obsessed with Ayoola's looks, just like Peter and Somto.

"Everyone is obsessed with her looks, Muhtar . . ."

He tells me *he* isn't, and I laugh. "You've never even seen her."

The door suddenly opens and I jump out of the chair. Tade walks into the room.

"I thought I'd find you here." He looks down at Muhtar's unconscious body. "You really care about this patient, don't you?"

"His family doesn't visit him as much as they used to."

"Yes, it's sad. But it's the way of things, I guess. Apparently he was a professor."

"Is."

"What?"

"Is. You said 'was.' Past tense. He isn't dead. Not yet, anyway."

"Oh! Yes. My bad. Sorry."

"You said you were looking for me?"

"I . . . I haven't heard from Ayoola." I sit back down in the chair. "I've called several times. She isn't picking up."

I have to admit, I am a little embarrassed. I haven't told Muhtar about Ayoola and Tade and I feel his pity strongly. I find myself blushing.

"She isn't great at returning calls."

"I know that. But this is different. I haven't spoken to her in two weeks . . . Can you talk to her for me? Ask her what I've done wrong."

"I'd rather not get involved . . ."

"Please, for me." He crouches and grabs my hand, drawing it to his heart and holding it there. "Please."

I should say no, but the warmth of his hands

around mine makes me feel dizzy, and I find myself nodding.

"Thank you. I owe you one."

With that, he leaves Muhtar and me to our devices. I feel too ridiculous to stay long.

CLEANER

Femi's family sent a cleaner to his home, to ready it to be put on the market—to move on, I guess. But the cleaner discovered a bloody napkin down the back of the sofa. It's all there on Snapchat, for the world to see that whatever happened to Femi, it did not happen of his own volition. The family is asking again for answers.

Ayoola tells me she may have sat there. She may have put the napkin on the seat to keep from staining the sofa. She may have forgotten about it . . .

"It's fine, if they ask me I'll just tell them he had a nosebleed." She is sitting in front of her dressing table tending to her dreadlocks and I am standing behind her, clenching and unclenching my fists.

"Ayoola, if you go to jail—"

"Only the guilty go to jail."

"First of all, that's not true. Second of all, you *killed* a man."

"*Defending* myself; the judge will understand that, right?" She pats her cheeks with blusher. Ayoola lives in a world where things must always go her way. It's a law as certain as the law of gravity.

I leave her to her makeup and sit at the top of the staircase, my forehead resting on the wall. My head feels as though there is a storm brewing inside it. The wall should be cool, but it is a hot day, so there is no comfort to be had there.

When I'm anxious, I confide in Muhtar—but he is in the hospital, and there is no one to share my fears with here. I imagine for the millionth time how it would go if I were to tell my mother the truth:

"Ma . . ."

"Hmmm."

"I want to talk to you about Ayoola."

"Are you people fighting again?"

"No, ma. I . . . there was an incident with erm Femi."

"The boy who is missing?"

"Well, he isn't missing. He is dead."

"Hey!!! Jésù ṣàánú fún wa o!"

"Yes . . . erm . . . but you see . . . Ayoola was the one who killed him."

"What is wrong with you? Why are you blaming your sister?"

"She called me. I saw him . . . I saw his body, I saw the blood."

"Shut up! Does this look like something you should be joking about?"

"Mum . . . I just . . ."

"I said shut up. Ayoola is a beautiful child with a wonderful temperament . . . Is that it? Is it jealousy that is making you say these horrible things?"

No, there is no point in involving my mother. It would be the death of her, or she would flat out deny that it could have happened. She would deny it even if she was the one who had been called upon to bury the body. Then she would blame me for it because I am the older sister—I am responsible for Ayoola.

That's how it has always been. Ayoola would break a glass, and I would receive the blame for giving her the drink. Ayoola would fail a class, and I would be blamed for not coaching her. Ayoola would take an apple and leave the store without paying for it, and I would be blamed for letting her get hungry.

I wondered what would happen if Ayoola were caught. If, for once, she were held responsible for her actions. I imagine her trying to blag her way out of it and being found guilty. The thought tickles me. I relish it for a moment, and then I force myself to set the fantasy aside. She is my sister. I don't want her to rot in jail, and besides, Ayoola being Ayoola, she would probably convince the court that she was innocent. Her actions were the fault of her victims and she had acted as any reasonable, gorgeous person would under the circumstances.

"Madam?"

I look up; the house girl is standing before me. She is holding a glass of water. I take it from her and hold it to my forehead. The glass is ice cold and I close my eyes and sigh. I thank her and she leaves as silently as she came.

There is banging, loud frenzied banging, in my head. I groan and roll over, unwilling to wake up. I am lying in my bed, fully dressed. It is dark and the banging is coming from the door and not my head. I sit up, trying to fight the still-strong effects of the painkiller I took. I walk to the door and unlock it. Ayoola pushes past me.

"Shit, shit, shit. They saw us!"

"What?"

"See!" Ayoola shoves her phone in my face and I take it from her. She is on Snapchat, and the video I am looking at has the face and shoulders of Femi's sister in the shot. Her makeup is impeccable but her look is somber.

"Guys, a neighbor has come forward. He didn't say anything before because he didn't think it mattered, but now that he's heard about the blood, he wants to tell us everything he knows. He says he saw two women leave my brother's apartment that night. Two! He couldn't see them too clearly, but he is pretty certain one of them is Ayoola—the babe who was dating my brother. Ayoola didn't tell us about a second woman with her . . . Why would she lie?"

I feel a chill race up and down my body.

Ayoola abruptly snaps her fingers. "You know what? I've got it!"

"Got what?"

"We'll tell them you were doing him behind my back."

"What?!"

"And I came in and discovered you and I ended it with him and you followed me out. But I didn't say anything 'cause I didn't want to bad-mouth someone who had . . ."

"You are unbelievable."

"Look, I know it paints you in a poor light, but it's better than the alternative."

I shake my head, hand her the phone and open the door for her to leave.

"Okay. Okay . . . how about we say you came over 'cause he called you to intervene between us. I wanted to end things and he thought you could convince me not to . . ."

"Or . . . how about, he wanted to end things with *you* and *you* thought I could intervene between the two of you and *you* were just too embarrassed to say."

Ayoola bites her lips. "Would people really believe that, though?"

"Get out."

BATHROOM

Alone in my room, I pace.

Femi's parents have the money needed to rouse the curiosity and professionalism of the police. And now they have a focus for their fear and confusion. They will want answers.

For the first time in my adult existence, I wish he was here. He would know what to do. He would be in control, every step of the way. He wouldn't allow his daughter's grievous error to ruin his reputation—he would have had this whole matter swept under the rug weeks ago.

But then it is doubtful Ayoola would have engaged in these activities had he been alive. The only form of retribution she ever feared was the one that came from him.

I sit down on my bed and think through the night of Femi's death. They fight, or something. Ayoola has her knife on her, since she carries it the way other women carry tampons. She stabs him, then leaves the bathroom to call me. She places the napkin on the sofa and sits on it. She waits for me. I arrive, we move the body. That is the moment we were most exposed. As far as I can tell, no one witnessed us moving the body, but I can't be 100 percent certain.

There is nothing out of place in my room, nothing to organize or clean. My desk has my laptop on it and my charger is neatly wound up and secured with a cable tie. My sofa faces the bed, its seat free of clutter, unlike the one in Ayoola's room that is basically drowning in dress patterns and different colored fabrics. My bed is turned down and the sheets are tightly tucked. My cupboard is shut, concealing clothes folded, hung and arranged according to color. But you can never clean a bathroom too many times, so I roll up my sleeves and head to the toilet. The cabinet under the sink is filled with everything required to tackle dirt and disease—gloves, bleach, disinfectant wipes, disinfectant spray, sponge, toilet bowl cleaner, all-purpose cleaner, multi-surface cleaner, bowl brush plunger and caddy, and odor-shield trash bags. I slip on the gloves and take out the multi-surface cleaner. I need some time to think.

QUESTIONS

They send the police over to question Ayoola. I guess Femi's family is done playing nice. The officers come to our house, and my mother asks me to bring them refreshments.

Minutes later, the three of us—Ayoola, Mum and I—and the two policemen are seated at the table. They are eating cake and drinking Coke, showering us with crumbs as they ask their questions. The younger one is stuffing his mouth as though he has not eaten in days, despite the fact that the chair can barely contain his girth.

"So he invited you over to his house?"

"Yes."

"And then your sister came?"

"Mm-hmm."

"Yes or no, ma."

"Yes."

I have asked her to keep her answers short and to the point, to avoid lying as much as she can, and to maintain eye contact.

When she informed me they were coming, I hustled Ayoola to our father's study.

Empty of books and memorabilia, it was just a musty space with a table, an armchair and a rug. It was gloomy, so I pulled back a curtain—the bright light revealed dust motes floating all around us.

"Why did you bring me here?"

"We need to talk."

"Here?" There were no distractions—no bed for Ayoola to lie on, no TV to draw her eyes and no material to fiddle with.

"Sit down." She frowned but complied. "When did you see Femi last?"

"What?! You know when I—"

"Ayoola, we need to be ready for these questions." Her eyes widened, and then she smiled. She leaned back.

"Don't lean back, you don't want to look too relaxed. An innocent person would still be tense. Why did you kill him?" She stopped smiling.

"Would they really ask that?"

"They may want to trip you up."

"I didn't kill him." She looked me straight in the eye as she said it.

Yes, I remember now, I didn't have to teach her to maintain eye contact. She was already a pro.

The younger policeman blushes. "How long had the two of you been dating, ma?"

"A month."

"That's not very long."

She says nothing, and I feel a sense of pride.

"But he wanted to break up with you?"

"Mm-hmm."

"He—wanted—to—break—up—with—you? Abi, was it the other way around?"

I wonder if Ayoola was right, that in my anger I had overlooked the unlikelihood that a man would willingly leave her side. Even now, we all pale beside her. She is dressed simply in a gray blouse and navy trousers, she has applied nothing but eyebrow pencil to her face and she isn't wearing jewelry—but it makes her look younger and fresher. When she gives the policemen an occasional smile she reveals her deep dimples.

I clear my throat and hope that Ayoola gets the message.

"Does it matter who wanted to end it?"

"Ma, if you wanted to end it, we need to know."

She sighs, and wrings her hands.

"I cared about him, but he wasn't really my type . . ." My sister is in the wrong profession. She should be in front of the camera, with the lights framing her innocence.

"What's your type, ma?" asks the younger one.

"So your sister came to mediate the issue?" his senior quickly adds.

"Yes. She came to help."

"And did she?"

"Did she what?"

"Did she help? Were you back together?"

"No . . . it was over."

"So, you and your sister went out together and left him there."

"Mmmm."

"Yes or no?"

"She has answered you na," interjects Mum. I feel another headache hovering. This is not the time for her mother-bear antics. She is puffed up now, having controlled herself for most of the interview. I imagine none of this makes sense to her. Ayoola gives her hand a gentle pat.

"It's okay, Mum, they're just doing their job. The answer is yes."

"Thank you, ma. What was he doing when you left him?"

Ayoola bites her lips, looks up and to the right. "He followed us to the door and shut it behind us."

"He was angry?"

"No. Resigned."

"Resigned, ma?"

She sighs. It is a masterful mix of weariness and sadness. We watch as she twirls a lock of hair around her finger. "I mean, he had accepted that things wouldn't work out between us."

"Ms. Korede, do you agree with that assessment? Did Mr. Durand accept his fate?"

I remember the body, half lying, half sitting on the

bathroom floor, and the blood. I doubt he had time to come to terms with his fate, let alone accept it.

"I imagine he was unhappy. But there was nothing he could have done to change her mind."

"And then you both drove home?"

"Yes."

"In the same car?"

"Yes."

"In Ms. Korede's car?" I dig my nails into my thighs and blink. Why are they so interested in my car? What could they possibly suspect? Did someone see us move the body? I attempt to slow my breathing without drawing attention to myself. No; no one saw us. If we had been seen carting around a body-shaped bundle, this interrogation would not be taking place in the comfort of our own home. These men didn't really suspect us. They had probably been paid to interview us.

"Yes."

"How did you get there, Ms. Ayoola?"

"I don't like to drive, I took an Uber."

They nod.

"Can we have a look at your car, Ms. Korede?"

"Why?" asks my mother. I should be moved that she feels the need to defend me, too; but instead I am furious at the fact that she suspects nothing, knows nothing. Why should her hands be clean, while mine become more and more stained?

"We just want to make sure we have covered all the bases."

"Why should we go through all this? My girls have done nothing wrong!" My mother rises from her seat as she delivers her heartfelt, misguided defense. The older policeman frowns and stands up, scraping his chair across the marble floor, and then nudges his partner to follow suit. Perhaps I will let this play out. Wouldn't the innocent be indignant?

"Ma, we will just have a quick look—"

"We have been accommodating enough. Please leave."

"Ma, if we have to, we will return with the necessary paperwork."

I want to speak, but the words won't leave my mouth. I'm paralyzed—all I can think of is the blood that was in the boot.

"I said leave," my mother stresses. She marches to the door, and they are forced to follow suit. They give Ayoola curt nods and leave the house. Mum slams the door behind them. "Can you believe those imbeciles?"

Ayoola and I don't answer. We are both reviewing our options.

BLOOD

They come the next day and take the car—my silver Ford Focus. The three of us stand on the doorstep, arms crossed, and watch them drive it away. My car is taken to a police station, in an area I never frequent, to be rigorously examined for evidence of a crime I did not commit, while Ayoola's Fiesta sits pretty in our compound. My eyes settle on her white hatchback. It has the shiny look of a newly washed vehicle. It has not been tainted with blood.

I turn to Ayoola.

"I'm using your car to go to work."

Ayoola frowns. "But what if I need to go somewhere during the day?"

"You can take an Uber."

"Korede," Mum begins carefully, "why don't you drive my car?"

"I don't feel like driving stick. Ayoola's car is fine."

I walk back into the house and head up to my room, before either of them has a chance to respond. My hands are cold, so I rub them on my jeans.

I cleaned that car. I cleaned it within an inch of its life.

If they find a dot of blood, it will be because they bled while they were searching. Ayoola knocks on my door and comes in. I pay no mind to her presence and pick up the broom to sweep my floor.

"Are you angry with me?"

"No."

"You could have fooled me."

"I just don't like being without a ride, is all."

"And it's my fault."

"No. It's Femi's fault for bleeding all over my boot."

She sighs and sits down on my bed, ignoring my "go away" face.

"You're not the only one suffering, you know. You act like you are carrying this big thing all by yourself, but I worry too."

"Do you? 'Cause the other day, you were singing 'I Believe I Can Fly.'"

Ayoola shrugs. "It's a good song."

I try not to scream. More and more, she reminds me of him. He could do a bad thing and behave like a model citizen right after. As though the bad thing had never happened. Is it in the blood? But his blood is my blood and my blood is hers.

FATHER

Ayoola and I are wearing aṣọ ẹbí. It is customary to wear matching ankara outfits for these types of functions. She chose the color—it is a rich purple ensemble. He hated the color purple, which makes her selection perfect. She also designed both our pieces—mine is a mermaid dress, flattering to my tall frame, and hers clings to her every curve. We both wear sunglasses to disguise the fact that our eyes are dry.

My mother weeps in church, bent double; her sobs are so loud and powerful, they rattle her body. I wonder what she is focusing on to bring about tears—her own frailty? Or maybe she is simply recalling what he did to her, to us.

I scan the aisles, and I see Tade searching for a place to sit.

"You invited him?" I hiss.

"I told him about it. He invited himself."

"Shit."

"What's the problem? You said I should be nice to him."

"I said you should clear things up. I didn't say you

should bring him into this further." My mother pinches me and I keep my mouth shut, but my body is shaking. Someone lays a kind hand on my shoulder, thinking me overcome with emotion. I am; just not the kind they think.

"Let us close our eyes and remember this man, because the years he spent with us were a gift from God." The voice of the priest is low, solemn. It is easy for him to say these things because he did not know the man. No one really knew him.

I close my eyes and mutter words of gratitude to whatever forces keep his soul captive. Ayoola searches for my hand and I take it.

After the service, people come to commiserate with us and to wish us well. A woman approaches me; she hugs me and will not let go. She starts to whisper: "Your father was a great man. He would always call me to check up on me and he helped with my school funds . . ." I am tempted to inform her that he had several girlfriends in various universities across Lagos. We had long since lost count. He once told me you had to feed the cow before you slaughtered it; it was the way of life.

I respond with a simple, "Yes, he paid for a lot of fees." When you have money, university girls are to men what plankton is to a whale. She smiles at me, thanks me and goes on her way.

The reception is what you would expect—a couple

of people we know, surrounded by people we don't remember but at whom we smile all the same. When I have some time to myself, I go outside and place another call to the police station to ask when they will return my car. Again, they give me the brush-off. If there was anything to be found, they will have found it by now, but the man on the other end of the line does not appreciate my logic.

I return in time to see Aunty Taiwo on the dance floor proving that she knows the latest steps to the latest hits. Ayoola is sitting in the middle of three guys, all of them competing for her attention. Tade has already left, and these guys are hoping to replace him for good. He had tried to be supportive, to stay by her side throughout, as a man should; but Ayoola was far too busy flitting this way and that, soaking in the spotlight. If he were mine, I wouldn't leave his side. I tear my eyes away from her and sip my Chapman.

MAGA

"Aunty, a man is here for you."

Ayoola is watching a movie on her laptop in my room. She could be watching it in her room, but she always seems to find her way to mine. She lifts her head to look at the house girl. I sit up immediately. It must be the police. My hands are cold.

"Who is it?"

"I don't know him, ma."

Ayoola shoots me a nervous look as she gets up from my bed, and I follow her out. The gentleman is seated on our sofa, and from where I stand, I can see that it is not the police and it is not Tade. The stranger holds a bouquet of roses in his hands.

"Gboyega!" She rushes down the steps and he catches her in one arm before swinging her around. They kiss.

Gboyega is a tall man with a protruding belly. His face is round and bearded, and his eyes are small and sharp. He also has at least fifteen years more life experience than Ayoola. If I squinted, I suppose I could see his attractiveness. But first I see the Bvlgari watch on his wrist and the Ferragamo shoes on his feet. He looks at me.

"Hello."

"Gboyega, this is Korede, my big sister."

"Korede, it is a pleasure to meet you. Ayoola tells me how you take care of her."

"You have me at a disadvantage. I haven't heard about you at all."

Ayoola laughs as if my comment were a joke, and she waves it away with a flick of her wrist.

"Gboye, you should have called."

"I know how you like surprises, and I just got into town." He leans over and they kiss again. I try not to gag. He hands her the flowers and she makes appropriate cooing sounds, even though the roses pale in comparison to the ones that Tade sent her. "Let me take you out."

"Okay, I'll need to get changed. Korede, will you keep Gboye company?" She has already dashed back upstairs before I can say no. Still, I set out to ignore her request and follow her up.

"So, you're a nurse?" he says to my retreating back. I stop and sigh.

"And you're married," I reply.

"What?"

"Your ring finger, the part where your ring would sit is lighter than the rest."

He shakes his head and smiles. "Ayoola knows."

"Yeah. I'm sure she does."

"I care about her. I want her to have the best of everything," he tells me. "I gave her the capital for her fashion business, you know, and paid for her course."

I'm surprised. She had told me that she paid for it herself—from the revenue from her YouTube videos. She had even piously lectured me for my lack of business sense. The more he talks, the more I realize that I am a maga—a fool who has been taken advantage of. Gboyega is not the problem, he is just another man, another person being used by Ayoola. If anything, he should be pitied. I want to tell him how much we have in common, though he boasts of the things he has done for her while I begin to resent the things that I have done. In solidarity, and to get him to be quiet, I offer him some cake.

"Sure, I love cake. Do you have tea?"

I nod. As I pass him, he winks at me.

"Korede." He pauses. "Ẹ jọ o, don't spit in my tea."

I give the house girl the necessary instructions and then cut through the kitchen and charge up the back stairs to interrogate Ayoola. She is applying eyeliner to her lower lids.

"What the hell is going on here?"

"This is why I didn't tell you. You are so judgmental."

"Are you serious? He tells me he paid for your fashion course. You said you raised the funds."

"I found a sponsor. Same difference."

"What about your . . . what about Tade?"

"What he doesn't know won't hurt him. Besides, can you blame me for wanting a little excitement in my life?

Tade can be so boring. And he is needy. Abeg, I need a break."

"What is wrong with you? When are you going to stop?!"

"Stop what?"

"Ayoola, you better send this man on his way, or I swear I'll—"

"You'll what?" She raises her chin and stares at me.

I don't do anything. I want to threaten her, to tell her that if she doesn't listen to me, she will have to deal with the consequences of her actions by herself for once. I want to shout and scream, but I would be screaming at a wall. I storm off to my bedroom. Thirty minutes later, she leaves the house with Gboyega.

She doesn't return till 1 a.m.

I don't sleep till 1 a.m.

FATHER

He often came home late. But I remember this night, because he wasn't alone. There was a yellow woman on his arm. We came out of my room because Mum was screaming, and there they were on the landing. My mother was wearing a camisole and her wrapper, her usual nightwear.

She never raised her voice to him. But that night, she was like a banshee; her fro was free of its bands and restraints, adding to the illusion of madness. She was Medusa and they were statues before her. She went to wrench the woman off his arm.

"Ẹ gbà mí o! Ṣ'o fẹ́ b'alé mi jẹ́? Ṣ'o fẹ́ yí mi lọ́rí ni? Olúwa k'ọjú sí mi!" She wasn't even screaming at her husband—it was the interloper whom she was mad at. I remember hissing at my mother, even though there were tears in my eyes. I remember thinking how silly she looked, so worked up as he stood tall and impassive before her.

He looked at his wife with indifference. "If you don't shut up now, I will deal with you," he informed her firmly.

Beside me, Ayoola held her breath. He always carried

out his threats. But this time my mother was oblivious, she was embroiled in a tug of war with the woman, who, though she looked like an adult to me then, I now know couldn't have been older than twenty. I understand now, too, that though my mother must have been aware of his indiscretions, having them take place in her home was more than she could bear.

"Free me!" the girl cried, trying to retrieve her wrist from my mother's ferocious grip.

Moments later he pulled our mother off her feet by her hair and slammed her against the wall. Then he struck her face. Ayoola whimpered and clutched me. The "woman" laughed.

"See, my boyfriend will not let you touch me."

My mother slid down the wall to the ground. They stepped over her and proceeded to his bedroom. We waited till the coast was clear and then ran to help her. She was inconsolable. She wanted to be left there to cry. She howled. I had to shake her.

"Mummy, please, let's go upstairs."

The three of us slept in my room that night.

The next morning, the banana-colored girl was gone and we sat around the table for breakfast, silent except for my father, who spoke loudly about the day ahead and congratulated his "perfect wife" on her excellent cooking. He wasn't sucking up, he had simply moved past the incident.

It wasn't long after that that Mother began to rely on Ambien.

RESEARCH

I stare at Gboyega's picture on Facebook. The man who stares back is a younger, slimmer version of him. I scroll through his pictures until I am satisfied that I know what kind of man he is. This is what I gather:

One well-dressed wife and three tall boys: the first two are now schooling in England, while the third is still in secondary school here. They reside in a townhouse on Banana Island—one of the most expensive estates in Lagos. He works in oil and gas. His photos are mostly of holidays in France, the U.S., Dubai, etc. They are every bit the typical upper-middle-class Nigerian family.

If his life is so blandly formulaic, I can see why he would be intrigued by Ayoola's unattainability and spontaneity. His captions go on and on about how wonderful his wife is, and how lucky he is to have her, and I wonder if his wife knows that her husband seeks out other women. She is good-looking in her own right. Even though she has birthed three sons and has left her youth behind, she has maintained a trim figure. Her face is expertly made up and her outfits flatter her and do justice to the money he must spend on her upkeep.

I have been calling Ayoola nonstop for half a day, trying to figure out where the hell she is. She left the house early in the morning and informed my mum that she was traveling. She didn't bother to tell me. Tade has been calling me just as much and I haven't answered. What am I to say? I have no idea where she is or what she is doing. Ayoola keeps her own counsel—until she needs me. The house girl brings me a glass of cold juice while I continue my research. It is burning hot outside, so I am spending my day off in the shadows of the house.

Gboyega's wife is not active on Facebook, but I find her on Instagram. Her posts about her husband and children are endless, broken up only by pictures of food and the occasional opinion on President Buhari's regime. Today's post is an old picture of herself and her husband on their wedding day. She is looking at the camera, laughing, and he is looking lovingly at her. The caption says:

> #MCM Oko mi, heart of my heart and father of my children. I thank God for the day you laid eyes on me. I did not know then you were afraid to speak to me, but I am glad you overcame that fear. I cannot imagine what my life would have been like without you. Thank you for being the man of my dreams. Happy anniversary bae. #bae #mceveryday #throwbackthursday #loveisreal #blessed #grateful

CAR

The police return my car to me—at the hospital. There is nothing subtle about their black uniforms and rifles. My fingernails dig into my palms.

"You couldn't have returned this to my house?" I hiss at them. From the corner of my eye, I see Chichi sidling closer.

"You better thank God we dey return am at all." He hands me a receipt. A torn piece of paper that has my license plate number, the date it was returned to me and the amount of 5,000 naira on it.

"What is this for?"

"Logistical and transportation costs." It is the younger one from the interview at our house; the one who was stumbling over himself for Ayoola's sake. His demeanor is not so clumsy now. I can tell he is ready for me to make a scene. Armed and ready. For a second, I wish Ayoola were beside me.

"Excuse me?!" They cannot be serious.

Chichi has almost reached my side. I cannot prolong this conversation. It occurs to me that they chose to drop it at my workplace for this exact reason. At home,

I would have had all the power. I could simply demand that they leave my compound. Here, I am at their mercy.

"Yes na. The cost of driving your car to and from our office is 5,000 naira."

I bite my lip. Angering them is not in my best interests; I need them to leave before they attract more attention. Every eye on either side of the hospital doors is on me, my car and these two geniuses.

I look at my car. It is dirty, covered in dust. And I can see a food container on the backseat. I can only imagine what the boot will look like. They have soiled my entire vehicle with their filthy hands, and no amount of cleaning will remove the memory of them.

But there is nothing I can do. I reach into my pocket and count out 5,000 naira.

"Did you find anything?"

"No," admits the older man. "Your car dey clean." I knew I had done a thorough job. I knew it would be clean. But hearing him say the words makes me want to weep with relief.

"Good morning, Officers!" Why is Chichi still here? Her shift ended thirty minutes ago. They return her cheerful good morning with a hearty one of their own. "Well done o," she tells them. "I see you brought my colleague's car back."

"Yes. Even though we are very busy people," the younger policeman stresses. He is leaning on my car, his fat hand on my bonnet.

"Well done. Well done. We are grateful. She had to be

managing her sister's car since." I hand over the money, they hand over my key. Chichi pretends she hasn't seen the exchange.

"Yes, thank you." It hurts to say this. It hurts to smile. "I understand you are both very busy. Don't let me keep you." They grunt and walk away. They will probably end up hailing an okada to take them back to their station. Beside me, Chichi is practically vibrating.

"Nawa o. What *happened*?"

"What happened to what?" I head back to the hospital, and Chichi follows.

"Why did they take your car na? I noticed since that you did not have your car, but I thought maybe it was with the mechanic or something. But I did not think the police had it!" She tries to whisper "police" and fails.

As we walk through the doors, so does Mrs. Rotinu. Tade is not in yet, so she will have to wait. Chichi grabs my hand and drags me into the X-ray room.

"So what happened?"

"Nothing. My car was involved in an accident. They were just checking it, for insurance purposes."

"And they took your car away just for that?"

"You know these police. Always working hard."

HEART

Tade looks like shit. His shirt is rumpled, he needs to shave and his tie is askew. No singing or whistling has escaped his lips in days. This is the power Ayoola has, and when I see Tade's suffering, I cannot help but be in awe of it.

"There is another guy," he tells me.

"There is?!" I'm overacting, my voice comes out as a squeak. Not that he notices. His head is down. He is half sitting on his desk, with his hands on either side, gripping it tightly, so I can make out the flexing and extending, the working together, the rippling of his body.

I drop the file I brought for him on the desk and reach out to touch him. His shirt is white. Not the sparkling white of the shirts Femi must have owned or of my nurses' uniform, but the white of a distracted bachelor. I could help Tade bleach his whites, if he would let me. I let my hand rest on his back and rub it. Does he find the gesture comforting? Eventually, he sighs.

"You're so easy to talk to, Korede."

I can smell his cologne mixed with his sweat. The

heat outside is seeping into the room and smothering the air from the AC.

"I like talking to you," I tell him. He raises his head and looks at me. We are only a step or two apart. Close enough to kiss. Are his lips as soft as they appear? He gives me a gentle smile, and I smile back.

"I like talking to you too. I wish . . ."

"Yes?" Has he started to see that Ayoola isn't right for him?

He looks down again, and I can't help myself.

"You're better off without her, you know," I tell him softly.

I feel him stiffen.

"What?" His voice is soft, but there is something beneath it that wasn't there before. Irritation? "Why would you say that about your sister?"

"Tade, she hasn't exactly been . . ."

He shrugs my hand off and pushes himself up and away from the desk, from me.

"You're her sister, you're supposed to be on her side."

"I'm always on her side. It's just that . . . she has many sides. Not all of them as pretty as the one that you see . . ."

"This is you being on her side, is it? She told me that you treat her like she is a monster, and I didn't believe her."

His words strike like arrows. He was *my* friend. Mine. He sought *my* counsel and *my* company. But now he looks at me as though I were a stranger and I hate him for it. Ayoola did what she always does in the company of men, but what is his excuse? I wrap my arms around my stomach, and turn my face from him so he can't see how my lips are trembling.

"I take it you believe her now?"

"I'm sure she is just grateful somebody does! It's no wonder she is always looking for attention from . . . men." He can barely say the last word, can barely think of Ayoola in the arms of another.

I laugh. I cannot help it. Ayoola has won so completely. She has traveled to Dubai with Gboyega (an update I got via text) and left Tade heartbroken, but somehow *I* am the witch.

I bet she forgot to mention that she has been instrumental in the death of at least three men. I take a deep breath so as not to say anything I'll regret. Ayoola is inconsiderate and selfish and reckless, but her welfare is and always has been my responsibility.

From the corner of my eye, I see that sheets from the file are askance. He must have shifted them when he got up from the desk. I use a finger to pull the file toward me and I pick it up, tapping it against the surface to line the papers up. Where is the merit in telling the truth? He doesn't want to hear it, he doesn't want to believe anything that comes out of my mouth. He just wants her.

"What she needs is your support and love. Then she will be able to settle down."

Why won't he shut up? The file is quaking in my

hands now and I can feel a migraine forming in a corner of my skull. He shakes his head at me. "You're her older sister. You should act like it. All I've seen you do is push her away." *Because of you* . . . But I say nothing. I've lost the urge to defend myself.

Was he always prone to lecturing this way? I drop the file on his table and walk past him quickly. I think I hear him call my name as I twist the doorknob, but it is drowned out by the sound of pounding in my head.

THE PATIENT

Muhtar is sleeping peacefully, waiting for me. I slip into his room and close the door.

"It's because she is beautiful, you know. That's all it is. They don't really care about the rest of it. She gets a pass at life." Muhtar allows me to rant. "Can you imagine, he said I don't support her, I don't love her . . . She let him think that. She told him that. After everything . . ."

I choke on my words, unable to finish them. Our silence is interrupted only by the rhythmic beeping of the monitor. I take several steadying breaths and check his chart. He is due for another bout of physiotherapy soon, so while I'm there I might as well take him through his exercises. His body is compliant as I move his limbs this way and that. My mind replays the scene with Tade over and over, cutting parts out, zooming in on others.

Love is not a weed,
It cannot grow where it please . . .

Words, from yet another of Femi's poems, come to me uninvited. I wonder what he would think of all of this. He hadn't been with Ayoola long. He would have figured her out given enough time. He was perceptive.

My stomach grumbles; the heart may be broken but the flesh needs to eat. I finish rolling Muhtar's ankles, smooth down his bedsheets and leave his room. Mohammed is mopping the floors of the corridor. The water he is using looks yellow and he hums to himself.

"Mohammed, change this water," I snap. He stiffens at the sound of my voice.

"Yes, ma."

ANGEL OF DEATH

"How was your trip?"

"It was fine . . . except . . . he died."

The glass I was drinking juice from slips out of my grip and shatters on the kitchen floor. Ayoola is standing in the doorway. She has been home all of ten minutes and I already feel as if my world is turning upside down.

"He . . . he died?"

"Yes. Food poisoning," she answers, shaking her dreadlocks. She has relocked them and placed beads on the ends, so as she moves they knock against each other and make a rattling sound. Her wrists are adorned with big gold bangles. Poison is not her style, and part of me wants to believe that this is a coincidence. "I called the police. They informed his family."

I crouch down to pick up some of the larger shards of glass. I think of the man's smiling wife on Instagram. Would she have the presence of mind to request an autopsy?

"We were in the room together and he suddenly starts to sweat and hold his throat. Then he starts to froth at the mouth. It was so scary." But her eyes are on fire, she is telling me a tale she thinks is fascinating. I don't want to talk to her, but she seems determined to share the details.

"Did you try to get him help?" I recall us, standing over our father, watching him die, and I know she did not try to get Gboyega help. She watched him. Maybe she didn't poison him, but she stood aside and let nature take its course.

"Of course. I called the emergency operator. But they didn't get there in time."

My eyes focus on the diamond comb sitting in her hair. The trip has been good to her. The Dubai air seems to have brightened her skin and she is wearing designer clothing from top to toe. Gboyega certainly wasn't stingy with his money.

"That's a shame." I search for a feeling greater than pity for this "family" man who died, but even that is sparse. I had never met Femi, but his fate affected me in a way this news does not.

"Yes. I'll miss him," she replies, absentmindedly. "Wait, I got you something." She dives into her handbag and begins rummaging, when the doorbell rings. She looks up expectantly and smirks. Surely, it can't be—but, you know, life. Tade walks through the door and she flings herself into his arms. He hugs her tight, burying his head in her hair.

"You naughty girl," he tells her and they kiss. Passionately.

I walk away quickly before he has a chance to realize

that there is a third person in the room. I'd hate to have to swap banalities with him. I lock myself in my room, sit on my bed cross-legged and stare into space.

Time passes. I hear a knock on my door.

"Ma, are you coming down to eat?" asks the house girl as she rocks back and forth on the balls of her feet.

"Who is at the dining table?"

"Mummy, sister Ayoola and Mr. Tade."

"Who sent you to call me?"

"I came myself, ma." No, of course they wouldn't think of me. My mum and Ayoola will be reveling in Tade's attention and Tade will . . . who cares what he will. I smile at the only person who seems to care if I have nourishment or not. From behind her small frame, laughter wafts toward me.

"Thank you, but I'm not hungry."

She shuts the door behind her as she leaves, shutting out the sound of happiness. At least Ayoola won't be in my space for a while. I use this opportunity to Google Gboyega's name. Sure enough, I find an article about his tragic passing—

Nigerian Dies on Dubai Business Trip

A Nigerian businessman died in Dubai after reportedly falling victim to a drug overdose.

The Foreign Office confirmed that Gboyega Tejudumi—who had been staying in the notorious Royal resort—died after having taken ill in his room.

Despite the efforts of the emergency services, he was pronounced dead at the scene.

There was no one else involved in the accident, according to the police . . .

I wonder how Ayoola convinced the police to keep her name out of the news. I wonder at the differences between a food poisoning and a drug overdose. I wonder what the chances are that the death of a person in the company of a serial killer would come about by chance.

Or perhaps the real question is, how confident am I that Ayoola only uses her knife?

I open other articles about Gboyega's death; I take in other lies. Ayoola never strikes unless provoked. But if she had a hand in Gboyega's death, if she was responsible, then why did she do it? Gboyega seemed infatuated. He was a cheat, but other than that he appeared harmless.

I think of Tade downstairs, smiling his signature smile and staring at Ayoola as though butter could not melt in her mouth. I couldn't bear to look into Tade's eyes, if he wasn't looking back at me. But haven't I done all I can to separate them? All I have to show for my trouble is judgment and scorn.

I switch off my laptop.

I write Gboyega's name in the notebook.

BIRTH

According to family lore, the first time I laid eyes on Ayoola I thought she was a doll. Mum cradled her before me and I stood on my toes, pulling Mum's arm down closer to get a better look. She was tiny, barely taking up space in the hammock Mum had created with her arms. Her eyes were shut and took up half her face. She had a button nose and lips that were permanently pursed. I touched her hair; it was soft and curly.

"Is she mine?"

Mum laughed, her body shaking, which stirred Ayoola awake. She gurgled. I stumbled backward in surprise and fell on my backside.

"Mummy, it talked! The doll talked!"

"She is not a doll, Korede. She is a baby, your baby sister. You're a big sister now, Korede. And big sisters look after little sisters."

BIRTHDAY

It's Ayoola's birthday. I allow her to begin posting again on her social media pages. Updates about Femi have dwindled. Social media has forgotten his name.

"Open my present first!" insists Mum. Ayoola obliges. It is tradition in our house that on a person's birthday, you open gifts from your family first thing in the morning. It took me a long time to figure out what to give her. I haven't exactly been in a giving mood.

Mum's gift is a dining set, for when Ayoola gets married. "I know Tade will ask soon," she announces.

"Ask what?" Ayoola replies, distracted by my present. I bought her a new sewing machine. She beams at me, but I can't smile back. Mum's words are turning my stomach.

"Ask for your hand in marriage!" Ayoola screws up her nose at the prediction. "It's time you, the both of you, start thinking about settling down."

" 'Cause marriage worked so well for you . . ."

"What did you say?"

"Nothing," I mutter. My mum eyes me but she did

not hear me, so she is forced to let it go. Ayoola gets up to change for her party, and I continue blowing up balloons. We picked gray and white, out of respect for Femi.

Earlier, I read a poem of his on his blog—

The African sun shines brightly.
Burning on our backs;
on our scalps,
on our minds—
Our anger has no cause, except if
the sun was a cause.
Our frustrations have no root, except if
the sun was a root.

I leave an anonymous message on the blog, suggesting that his poems be collected and made into an anthology. I hope his sister or a friend comes across the message.

Ayoola and I don't really have friends in the traditional sense of the word. I think you have to accept someone into your confidence, and vice versa, to be able to call them a friend. She has minions, and I have Muhtar. The minions begin to flood in around 4 p.m.; the house girl lets them in, and I direct them to the food piled on the living room table. Someone puts on music, and people nibble at the snacks. But all I can think about is whether or not Tade will use this as an opportunity to try to secure Ayoola forever. If I thought she loved him,

I think I could be happy for them. I could, I think. But she doesn't love him and for some reason he is blind to that fact; or he doesn't care.

It's 5 p.m. and Ayoola hasn't come down yet. I'm wearing the quintessential black dress. It's short and has a flared skirt. Ayoola said she would be wearing black too, but I am pretty sure she has changed her mind at least a dozen times by now. I resist the urge to go and check on her, even when I am asked for the hundredth time where she is.

I hate house parties. People forget the etiquette they would apply if they visited your house on a normal day. They leave their paper plates on any and every surface; they spill drinks and walk away; they dip their hands in snack bowls, take some and put some back; they look for places to make out. I pick up a set of paper cups that someone has left on a footstool and put it in a garbage bag. I'm just about to fetch some surface cleaner when the doorbell rings: Tade.

He looks . . . he is wearing jeans and a white T-shirt that hugs his body, and a gray blazer. I can't help but stare at him.

"You look nice," he tells me. I suppose complimenting my appearance is supposed to be an olive branch. It shouldn't affect me. I've stayed out of his way, I've kept my head down. I don't want his casual compliment to touch me; but I feel a lightness inside me. I squeeze the muscles of my face to keep a smile from bursting through. "Look, Korede, I'm sor—"

"Hey." The "hey" comes from behind me, and I turn around to see Ayoola. She is wearing a fitted maxi dress so close to the color and shade of her skin that in the dim lighting she looks almost naked, with gold earrings, gold heels and the bracelet Tade gave her to top it off. I can detect a smattering of light gold bronzer on her skin.

Tade walks past me and kisses her gently on the lips. Love or not, they are a very attractive couple; on the outside, at least. He hands her a gift and I slide closer so I can see what it is. It's a small box, but too long and narrow to be a ring. Tade looks my way, and I make like a bee and act busy. I head back to the center of the party and start picking up paper plates again.

I see flashes of Tade and Ayoola throughout the night—laughing together by the punch bowl, kissing on the stairs, feeding each other cake on the dance floor, until I can take it no longer. I grab a shawl from a drawer and head out of the house. It's still warm, but I wrap my arms around myself under the fabric. I need to talk to someone, anyone; someone besides Muhtar. I considered therapy once, but Hollywood has revealed that therapists have a duty to break confidence if the life of the patient or someone else is at stake. I have a feeling that if I were to talk about Ayoola, that confidence would be broken in five minutes. Isn't there an option where no one dies and Ayoola doesn't have to be incarcerated? Perhaps I could see a therapist and just leave the murders out of it. I could fill plenty of sessions just talking about Tade and Ayoola and how seeing them together turns me inside out.

"Do you like him?" she had asked me. No, Ayoola. I love him.

HEAD NURSE

As soon as I walk into the hospital, I head to Dr. Akigbe's office, as per his email request. As usual, his email was abrupt, mysterious, designed to keep the receiver on their toes. I knock.

"Come in!" His voice is like a hammer against the door.

At the moment Dr. Akigbe, St. Peter's oldest and most senior doctor, is staring at his computer screen, scrolling down with his mouse. He doesn't say anything to me, so I sit down of my own accord and wait. He stops scrolling and raises his head.

"Do you know when this hospital was founded?"

"Nineteen seventy-one, sir." I lean back in my seat and sigh. Is it really possible that he called me here to lecture me on the hospital's history?

"Excellent, excellent. I wasn't here then, of course. I'm not that old!" He laughs at his own joke. He is, of course, that old. He just happened to be working elsewhere at the time. I clear my throat, in hopes of deterring him from beginning a story I have heard a thousand times before. He stands up, revealing his full six-foot-three frame and stretches. I know what he is doing. He's going to bring out the photo album. He will show me pictures of the hospital in its earliest days and of the three founders he can never stop talking about.

"Sir, I have to, Ta . . . Dr. Otumu wants me to assist with a PET scan."

"Right, right." He is still scanning the bookshelf for the album.

"I'm the only nurse on the floor trained to assist with a PET scan, sir," I say pointedly. Perhaps it is too much to hope my words will hurry him, but whatever he wants to say to me, I'd rather not wait an hour to hear it. To my surprise, he spins around and beams at me.

"And that is why I called you here!"

"Sir?"

"I have been watching you for some time." He demonstrates this with his forefinger and middle finger directed at his eyes, and then at me. "And I like what I see. You are meticulous and you are passionate about this hospital. Frankly, you remind me of me!" He laughs again. It sounds like a dog barking.

"Thank you, sir." His words warm me on the inside, and I smile at him. I was just doing my job, but it is gratifying to have my efforts acknowledged.

"Needless to say, you were a shoe-in for the position of head nurse!" Head nurse. It's certainly a role that suits me. After all, I have been doing the work of a head nurse for some time now. Tade mentioned that I was being considered for the role and I think of the celebratory dinner he promised we would have. That's null and void now, I guess. I don't have Tade's friendship and Femi is probably swelling to three times his size, but I am now the head nurse of St. Peter's Hospital. It has a nice ring to it.

"I'm honored, sir."

COMA

When I head to the reception desk, Chichi is still hovering. Perhaps there is a man at home she is loath to return to. She is talking animatedly to a group of staff members who are barely listening. I catch the words "miracle" and "coma."

"What's going on?" I ask.

"You haven't heard?"

"Heard what?"

"Your best friend is awake!"

"Awake? Who? Yinka?"

"No. Mr. Yautai! He is awake!"

I'm running before I even think to answer. I leave Chichi standing by the nurses' station and hurry to the third floor. I would rather have heard the news from Dr. Akigbe, so I could have asked the pertinent neurological questions, but considering that he spied yet another opportunity to lecture on the hospital's history, it is no surprise that he failed to mention it. Or perhaps he didn't mention it because it is not true at all, and Chichi misunderstood . . .

Muhtar's family is crowded around his bed, so I don't

immediately see him. His wife, whose slender frame is carved in my memory, and a tall man who I guess is his brother, have their backs to me. They are not touching, but their bodies are leaning toward each other as if pulled together by some force. Perhaps they have been comforting each other one time too often.

Facing the door, and now me, are his children. His two sons stand rod straight—one crying silently—while his daughter holds her newborn in her arms, angling the baby so her father can see. It is this gesture that finally forces me to face the reality of his consciousness. Muhtar has rejoined the land of the living.

I back away from the family reunion, but then I hear his voice. "She is beautiful."

I have never heard his voice before. When I met him, he was already in the coma and I had imagined his voice to be rich and heavy. In reality, he hasn't spoken in months, so his voice is high-pitched, weak, almost a whisper.

I turn and bump into Tade.

"Whoa," he says. He stumbles backward and catches himself.

"Hey," I say, distracted, my mind still back in Muhtar's room. Tade looks over my shoulder at the scene.

"So, Mr. Muhtar is awake?"

"Yeah, it's great," I manage.

"I'm sure it is thanks to you."

"Me ke?"

"You kept the guy going. He was never forgotten, never neglected."

"He doesn't know that."

"Maybe not, but you can't anticipate what stimuli the brain will respond to."

"Yes."

"Congratulations, by the way."

"Thanks." I wait, but he makes no mention of his promise that we would celebrate the promotion.

I sidestep him and continue down the corridor.

Just as I return to reception, there is a scream. The waiting patients look around themselves in surprise, while Yinka and I run toward the sound. It's coming from room 105. Yinka flings open the door and we burst in to find Assibi and Gimpe locked together. Gimpe has Assibi in a headlock and Assibi is clawing at Gimpe's breasts. They freeze when they see us. Yinka begins to laugh.

"Ye!" she cries after the laughter is gone from her.

"Thank you, Yinka," I say pointedly.

She stands there, still grinning.

"Thank you," I say again. The last thing I need is Yinka adding fuel to an already raging flame.

"What?"

"I can handle it from here."

For a moment I think she's going to argue, but then she shrugs. "Fine," she mutters. She takes one more look at Assibi and Gimpe, smirks, then flounces from the room. I clear my throat.

"You stand over there, you stand over there." When they have taken their places far away from each other, I remind them that this is a hospital and not a bar by the side of the road.

"I should have you both fired."

"No, ma."

"Please, ma."

"Explain to me what was so serious that you had to fight physically." They don't respond. "I'm waiting."

"It's Gimpe. She has been trying to steal my boyfriend."

"Oh?"

"Mohammed is not your boyfriend!" Mohammed? Seriously? Perhaps I should have left Yinka to handle this. Now that I think of it, she probably guessed what was going on.

Mohammed is a terrible cleaner with poor personal hygiene and yet he has somehow gotten these two women to fall for him, creating drama inside the hospital. He should really be fired. I would not miss him.

"I don't care whose boyfriend Mohammed is. You people can eye each other from afar or burn each other's houses down, but when you enter this hospital, you will behave in a professional manner or risk your jobs. Do you understand?"

They mumble something that sounds like *mmmshhh shingle hghate bchich*.

"Do you understand?"

"Yes, ma."

"Excellent. Please get back to work."

When I return to reception, I find Yinka leaning back, eyes closed, mouth open.

"Yinka!" I slam a clipboard down on the countertop, startling her awake. "If I catch you sleeping again, I will write you up."

"Who died and made you head nurse?"

"Actually," mutters Bunmi, "they promoted her this morning."

"What?"

"There will be a meeting about it later in the day," I add.

Yinka doesn't speak.

THE GAME

It's raining, the sort of rain that wrecks umbrellas and renders a raincoat useless. We are stuck in the house—Ayoola, Tade and I. I try to avoid them, but Ayoola collars me as I walk through the living room.

"Let's play a game!"

Tade and I sigh.

"Count me out," I say.

"Why don't *we* play, just the two of us?" Tade suggests to Ayoola. I ignore the stab to my heart.

"No. It's a three-or-more-person game. It has to be all of us or none of us."

"We can play checkers, or chess?"

"No. I want to play Cluedo."

If I were Tade, I'd tell her to stuff the Cluedo up her entitled be—

"I'll go get it." She jumps up and leaves Tade and me in the room together. I don't want to look at him, so I stare out the window at the washed-out scenery. The streets in the estate are empty, everyone has taken refuge indoors. In the Western world you can walk or dance in the rain, but here, the rain will drown you.

"I may have been a bit harsh the other day," he says. He waits for me to respond, but I can think of nothing to say. "I've been told sisters can be very . . . mean to one another."

"Who told you that?"

"Ayoola."

I want to laugh, but it comes out like a squeak.

"She really looks up to you, you know." I finally look at him. I look into his innocent light brown doe eyes and I wonder if I was ever like that, if I ever had that kind of innocence. He is so wonderfully normal and naïve. Maybe his naïveté is as alluring to Ayoola as it is to me—I suppose ours was beaten out of us. I open my mouth to answer, and Ayoola hops back onto the couch. She is holding the board game close to her chest. His eyes forget me and focus on her.

"Tade, have you played before?"

"No."

"Okay, you play to find out who the murderer was, in what room the murder took place and with what weapon. Whoever figures it out first, wins!"

She passes the rule book to him and winks at me.

SEVENTEEN

Ayoola was seventeen the first time and scared out of her wits. She called me and I could barely make sense of her words.

"You what?"

"I . . . the knife . . . it's . . . there's blood everywhere . . ." Her teeth were chattering as though she were cold. I tried to control my rising panic.

"Ayoola, slow down. Take a deep breath. Where are you bleeding?"

"I . . . I'm not . . . Somto. It's Somto."

"You were attacked?"

"I . . ."

"Where are you? I'll call—"

"No! Come alone."

"Ayoola, where are you?"

"Will you come alone?"

"I'm not a doctor."

"I won't tell you, unless you promise to come alone." So I promised.

When I got to the apartment Somto was already dead.

His trousers were around his ankles and the shock on his face mirrored mine.

"You . . . you did this?"

Back then I was too scared to hang about and clean, so we torched the room. I never even considered putting Ayoola at the mercy of the police. Why take the risk that her cry of self-defense might go unheard?

Somto had a studio apartment to himself that overlooked the water—the very water that led into the third mainland bridge lagoon. We took the diesel he was keeping for his generator, poured it over his body, lit a match and fled. The other tenants ran out of the block quickly when the fire alarm went off, so there was no collateral damage. Somto was a smoker; it was all the proof the university needed.

Murderer—Ayoola; Place—Studio Apartment; Weapon—Knife.

MANEATER

Ayoola wins Cluedo, but only because I am forced to keep explaining the rules to Tade to prevent him from falling into the traps she is so adept at setting.

I had convinced myself that if Tade could win here . . . then maybe . . .

"You're a pro at this," he tells her, squeezing her thigh. "Hey, I'm hungry. I wouldn't mind some of that cake. Do you have any left?"

"Ask Korede na."

"Oh. Korede bakes too?"

She raises her eyebrows and glances at me. I meet her eyes and wait.

"You think I bake?"

"Yes . . . I had your pineapple upside-down cake."

"Did Korede tell you I baked that?"

He frowns. "Yes . . . Wait, no . . . It was your mum."

She smiles at him, as if sorry that he was deceived.

"I can't bake to save my life," she states plainly. "Korede made apple crumble this morning, would you like that?"

"Oh. Okay, sure."

Ayoola calls for the house girl and tells her to bring the apple crumble with custard and side plates. Five minutes later, she is dishing out hefty portions. I push mine away, feeling nauseous. Tade takes a bite of his, closes his eyes and smiles. "Korede, this is heavenly."

AWAKE

I haven't gone to Muhtar's room since he came out of his coma. It's the end of that era. I can no longer talk to him with impunity and I was not the nurse allocated to attend to him in the first place.

"Korede."

"Hmmm."

"The patient in room 313 would like to see you."

"Muhtar? Why?"

Chichi shrugs. "Better go and ask him."

I consider ignoring the summons, but he'll soon be walking around the floor as part of his physiotherapy, so I know it is only a matter of time before I see him. I knock on his door.

"Come in."

He is sitting up in bed with a book in his hands, which he sets down beside him. He looks at me expectantly. There are heavy rings around his eyes, but his pupils are focused and sharp. He seems to have aged since he woke up.

"I'm Nurse Korede." His eyes widen.

"You're the one."

"The one?"

"The one who visited me."

"Oh, they told you?"

"Who?"

"The nurses."

"The nurses? No, no. I remember."

"You remember what?" The room is cold; my hands are tingling, their temperature dropping.

"I remember your voice. You talking to me."

My skin is dark, but I am certain all the blood has rushed to my feet, rendering me ghostlike. What happened to all that research that established the unlikelihood that comatose patients were aware of their surroundings? Yes, Tade had been convinced that my visits were doing some good, but I had never thought Muhtar could actually hear me.

"You remember me talking to you?"

"Yes."

"Do you remember what I said?"

MARKET

When I was ten, my mum lost me in the market.

We went to buy tomatoes, bitter leaf, crayfish, onions, ata rodo, tàtàsé, plantain, rice, chicken and beef. I was holding the list, but I had already memorized everything and I chanted it under my breath.

Mum was holding Ayoola's hand and I walked behind them. My eyes were focused on my mother's back, so I wouldn't lose them in the sea of people pushing and shoving their way between the stalls. Ayoola saw something, a lizard perhaps, and decided to chase it. She pulled her hand from my mother's grip and ran. My mother, acting on instinct, ran after her.

It took me a second to react. At the time, I didn't know Ayoola had run off. One minute my mother was walking quickly but steadily in front of me, the next she was hightailing it away without me.

I tried to follow, but I lost her immediately and stopped running. Suddenly, I was in an unfamiliar place, surrounded by threatening strangers. I feel now much the way I felt then. Uncertain, afraid and very sure that something bad is going to happen to me.

MEMORY

Muhtar frowns, knitting together his brows, and then he shrugs.

"It's very patchy."

"What do you remember?"

"Would you like to sit down?" He gestures at a seat and I oblige. I need to keep him talking. I told this man almost every secret I had, convinced that he would take those secrets to the grave, but now he is giving me a shy smile and trying to meet my eye.

"Why did you do it?"

"Do what?" I ask, but I don't recognize my voice.

"Visit me. You don't know me, and I get the impression the visits from my family had dwindled to almost nothing."

"It was tough for them, seeing you like that."

"You don't have to make excuses for them." We are both silent after that, not sure what to say. "I have a granddaughter now."

"Congratulations."

"The father says she isn't his."

"Oh. Curious."

"Are you married?"

"No."

"Good. Marriage isn't what they say it is."

"You were saying you remembered something?"

"Yes. It's amazing, isn't it? You think the whole body is in hibernation, but the brain is still working, still garnering information. Really fascinating." Muhtar is far more talkative than I thought he would be and he gestures quite wildly when he talks. I can imagine him in front of a roomful of youths, lecturing them on things they couldn't care less about, but going at it with passion and gusto.

"So, you remember a lot, then?"

"No. Not a lot. I know you like popcorn with syrup. You said I should try it sometime."

My breath catches in my throat. No one else here would know that except Tade, and Tade isn't one to play tricks.

"Is that all?" I ask quietly.

"You seem nervous. Are you okay?"

"I'm fine."

"I have some water here, if you . . ."

"Really, I'm okay. Is there anything else?"

He appraises me, cocking his head. "Oh yes, I recall you saying that your sister is a serial killer."

MADNESS

What led me to confide in a body that still had breath left in it?

An unwanted thought enters my mind—a means to an end. I squash the thought, meet his gaze and laugh. "Who did I say she killed?"

"I don't quite remember that."

"Well, it's to be expected. Coma patients usually have a hard time separating their dream world from the real world."

He nods. "I was thinking the same thing."

He doesn't seem convinced, though, or perhaps my fear is making me read too much into his tone of voice. He is still staring at me, trying to make sense of things. I have to remain professional.

"Have you been experiencing any headaches?"

"No . . . I haven't."

"Good. Finding it hard to sleep?"

"Sometimes . . ."

"Hmmm . . . Well, if you begin to suffer hallucinations . . ."

"Hallucinations?!"

"Don't be alarmed, just let the doctor know."

He looks alarmed, and I feel a little guilty. I stand up.

"Rest, and if you need anything, press the button beside you."

"Would you mind staying a bit longer? You have a pleasant voice."

His face is narrow and stiff. His eyes are the most expressive thing about him. I stand, pushing the chair back in its corner and his eyes follow me as I move around straightening things that are already in their place. They put me on edge.

"Sorry, sir, I have to return to work."

"Aren't you working by being here?"

"I'm not the nurse designated to care for you." I force a smile and pretend to glance at his notes, and then head to the door. "I'm glad you're feeling better, Mr. Yautai," I say, and leave the room.

Three hours later, Bunmi informs me that Muhtar has requested me as his nurse. Yinka, who *is* his nurse, shrugs, not caring one chit.

"He has creepy eyes anyway."

"To whom did he make the request?" I ask.

"Dr. 'Put the Patient First.'" Dr. Akigbe. The chance that Dr. Akigbe will allow Muhtar's request is very, very high. He loves to grant patient requests that require nothing from him.

I sink into the chair at the reception desk and consider my options, but none of them are ideal. I imagine writing his name in the notebook. I wonder if this is how it is for Ayoola—one minute she is giddy with happiness and good cheer, and the next minute her mind is filled with murderous intent.

ASLEEP

I dream of Femi. Not the inanimate Femi. The Femi whose smile was plastered all over Instagram and whose poetry is memorialized in my mind. I have been trying to understand how he became a victim.

He was arrogant, there's no doubt about it. But handsome, talented men usually are. His tone on his blog was abrupt and cynical and he didn't appear to suffer fools lightly. But as though at war with himself, his poetry was playful and romantic. He was . . . complex. The sort of man who shouldn't have fallen under Ayoola's spell.

In my dream, he leans back in his chair and asks me what I'm going to do.

"Do about what?"

"She's not going to stop, you know."

"She was defending herself."

"You don't really believe that," he chides, shaking his head feebly.

He stands up and starts to walk away from me. I follow him, because what else can I do? I want to wake up, but I also want to see where Femi will take me. It turns out, he wants to visit the place where he died. We stare at his body, the utter helplessness of it all. Beside him, on the floor, is the knife she carries with her and spills blood with. She had hidden it before I got there, but in my dream I see it as clear as day.

He asks me if he could have done anything differently.

"You could have seen her for what she was."

ICE CREAM

Her name is Peju.

She is hovering outside our compound and makes her move the moment I pull out of the gate. I don't immediately recognize her, but I stick my head out of the window to see what she wants.

"What did you do to him?"

"Sorry?"

"Femi. What did you do to Femi?" I realize then who she is. I have seen her, too many times to count, on Instagram. She is the one who has been posting about Femi, the one who called Ayoola out on Snapchat. She has lost a lot of weight and her pretty eyes are red. I try to remain impassive.

"I can't help you."

"Can't? Or won't? I just want to know what happened to him." I attempt to drive on, but she opens my door. "The worst thing is not knowing." Her voice breaks.

I turn off the engine and climb out of the car. "I'm sorry, but—"

"Some people are saying he probably up and left the

country, but he wouldn't do that, and he wouldn't worry us like this . . . If we knew . . ."

I feel a strong urge to confess to her, to tell her what happened to her brother so that she won't have to go through life wondering. I think up the words in my head—*Sorry, my sister stabbed him in the back and I masterminded throwing his body in the water*. I think of how it would sound. I think of what would happen after.

"Look, I'm really—"

"Peju?"

Peju's head snaps up to see my sister coming down the drive.

"What are you doing here?" Ayoola asks.

"You're the one who saw him last. I know there is something you're not saying. Tell me what happened to my brother."

Ayoola is wearing dungarees—she is the only person I know who can still pull those off—and she is licking ice cream, probably from the parlor around the corner. She pauses the licking, not because she is moved by Peju's words, but because she is aware that it is proper to pause whatever one is doing when in the presence of someone who is grieving. I spent three hours explaining that particular etiquette to her one Sunday afternoon.

"You think he is . . . dead?" asks Ayoola in a low soft voice.

Peju starts weeping. It is as though Ayoola's question knocks down a dam that she has been doing her best to keep up. Her cries are deep and loud. She gulps in air and her body shudders. Ayoola takes another lick of the ice cream and then she pulls Peju into an embrace with her free arm. She rubs Peju's back as she cries.

"It'll be alright. It'll be alright in the end," Ayoola murmurs to her.

Does it matter who Peju is getting comfort from? What's done is done. So what if it is only her brother's killer who can talk candidly about the possibility of his death? Peju needed to be released from the crushing burden of hope that Femi could still be alive and Ayoola was the only one willing to do it.

Ayoola continues to pat Peju on her back as she stares resignedly at the ice cream, the one she can no longer lick, as it drip drips onto the road.

SECRET

"Korede, can I talk to you for a sec?"

I nod and follow Tade into his office. As soon as the door is shut, he beams at me. My face flushes and I cannot help but smile back.

He looks particularly good today—he has recently had his hair cut. He is usually quite conservative with his hair, trimming it down almost to the scalp, but he has been growing it out recently, and now he has a short back and sides with the middle left an inch high. It suits him.

"I want to show you something, but you have to promise to keep it a secret."

"Okay . . ."

"Promise."

"I promise I'll keep it a secret."

He hums as he goes to his drawer and fishes something out. It is a box. A ring box.

"Who?" I squeak. As if there was ever any doubt who the ring is for. And who it isn't for.

"Do you think she'll like it?"

The ring is a two-carat princess cut diamond with a

precious-stone setting. You would have to be blind not to like it.

"You want to propose to Ayoola," I state, so we are all on the same page.

"Yes. Do you think she'll say yes?"

Finally, a question I don't know the answer to. I blink back hot tears and I clear my throat. "Isn't this too soon?"

"When you know, you know. You'll understand one day, Korede, when you're in love."

I surprise myself by laughing. It starts off as a gasp, then a giggle, then uncontrollable tear-jerking laughter. Tade is staring at me, but I can't stop. When I finally calm down, he asks, "What's so funny?"

"Tade . . . what do you like about my sister?"

"Everything."

"But if you had to be specific."

"Well . . . she is . . . she is really special."

"Okay . . . but what makes her special?"

"She is just so . . . I mean, she is beautiful and perfect. I've never wanted to be with someone this much."

I rub my forehead with my fingers. He fails to point out the fact that she laughs at the silliest things and never holds a grudge. He hasn't mentioned how quick she is to cheat at games or that she can hemstitch a skirt without even looking at her fingers. He doesn't know her best features or her . . . darkest secrets. And he doesn't seem to care.

"Put your ring away, Tade."

"What?"

"This is all . . ." I perch on his desk and try to find the words. "This is all just fun and games to her."

He sighs, and shakes his head. "People change, Korede. I know she cheated on me, and all that, but that's 'cause she hasn't known real love. And that's what I can give her."

"She will hurt you." I go to put my hand on his shoulder, but he shrugs me off.

"I can handle . . ."

How can a man be so obtuse? The frustration I feel is like a gas bubble in my chest, and I cannot control the need to burp.

"No. I mean it—she will hurt you. Physically! She has hurt people—guys—before." I try to illustrate my point with my hands, strangling thin air.

There is a moment of silence while he considers what I've said and I consider the fact that I said it. I drop my hands. I should stop talking now. I have told him as much as I can. He's on his own from here.

"Is it because you don't have someone?" he asks.

"Excuse me?"

"Why don't you want Ayoola to move forward in life? It's like you want her to depend on you for the rest of her days." He shakes his head in disappointment and I have to check every urge to scream. I dig my nails into my palm. I've never held Ayoola back; if anything, I've given her a future.

"I don't . . ."

"It's like you don't want her to be happy."

"She's killed before!" I shout, regretting the words as soon as I have uttered them. Tade shakes his head again, marveling at how low I am willing to stoop.

"She told me about the guy who died. Said you blame her for it." I'm tempted to ask him which guy he is referring to, but I can see this is a battle that I cannot win. I lost before I even knew it had started. Ayoola may not be here, but Tade is like a puppet, speaking her words.

"Look." His voice softens as he changes tack. "She really wants your approval, and all she gets from you is judgment and disdain. She lost someone she loved and all you do is make her feel responsible. I would never have thought you could be so cruel. I thought I knew you, Korede."

"No. You know nothing about me, or the woman you are about to propose to. And by the way, Ayoola would never wear a ring less than three carats." He stares at me as though I'm speaking another language, the ring box still clutched in his hand. What a waste of time this all was.

I glance at him over my shoulder as I open the door. "Just watch your back." She had warned me: *He isn't deep. All he wants is a pretty face.*

FRIEND

As I approach the reception desk, Yinka looks up from her phone.

"Oh good, it's you. I was afraid I would have to come and find you."

"What do you want?"

"Excuse you . . . *I* don't want anything, but coma guy has been asking for you nonstop."

"His name is Muhtar."

"Whatever." Yinka leans back and resumes playing Candy Crush. I turn on my heel and make my way to room 313.

He is sucking on an àgbálùmọ̀, sitting in one of the armchairs. Another nurse must have set him up there for a change of scenery. He smiles when I walk in.

"Hello!"

"Hi."

"Please sit, sit."

"I can't really stay long." I'm not in the mood for chatting, my conversation with Tade is still ringing in my ears.

"Sit."

I sit. He looks much better. His hair has been cut, and he appears to have put on a bit of weight. His color looks better, too. I tell him as much.

"Thank you. It's a wonder what being conscious can do for one's health!" He laughs at himself, then stops. "Are you okay? You look a bit pale."

"I'm fine. What can I help you with, Mr. Yautai?"

"Please, there's no need for formalities. Call me Muhtar."

"Okay . . ."

He stands up and grabs a paper bag off the coffee table; he hands it to me. Popcorn with syrup drizzled all over it. It looks delicious.

"You didn't have to do this."

"I wanted to. It's the least I can do to thank you."

The hospital does not allow us to accept gifts from patients, but I do not want to offend him by rejecting his attempt at gratitude. I thank him, take the bag and set it to one side.

"I've been thinking some more about my memories, and some things are a little clearer to me," he begins.

Honestly, I am too tired for this. I can take only so much in a day. Perhaps he will remember everything I told him, including where the bodies are, and it will all be over.

"Let's say for argument's sake that one knew someone who had committed a gross crime. Someone dear to one. What would one do?" He pauses.

I sit back in my chair and appraise him. I must choose

my words wisely, since I have carelessly given this man the tools he needs to have my sister and me thrown into jail, and I have no idea what his angle is. "One would be duty bound to report it."

"One would be, yes, but most of us wouldn't, would we?"

"Wouldn't we?"

"No, because we are hardwired to protect and remain loyal to the people we love. Besides, no one is innocent in this world. Why, go up to your maternity ward! All those smiling parents and their newborns? Murderers and victims. Every one of them. 'The most loving parents and relatives commit murder with smiles on their faces. They force us to destroy the person we really are: a subtle kind of murder.'"

"That's quite . . ." I can't complete the sentence. The words trouble me.

"It's a quote by Jim Morrison. I cannot lay claim to such wisdom." He continues to suck on the àgbálùmọ̀. He is quiet, waiting for me to speak.

"Are you going to tell anyone about . . . this?"

"I doubt the words of a coma patient hold much water out there." He gestures with his thumb to the door that separates us from the world outside.

Neither of us says anything. I focus on slowing down my heart rate. Without my permission, tears run down my face. Muhtar keeps mum. He allows me the time to appreciate that there is someone who knows what I'm dealing with, that there is someone on my side.

"Muhtar, you know enough to have us put away forever. Why do you keep this secret?" I ask him as I wipe my face dry.

He sucks on another àgbálùmọ̀ and winces at the sharpness of the flavor.

"Your sister, I do not know. I hear from your colleagues that she is very lovely, but I have not seen her for myself and so do not care about her. You, I know." He points to me. "You, I care about."

"You don't know me."

"I know you. I woke up because of you—your voice calling to me. I still hear you in my dreams . . ."

He is waxing lyrical. It feels like I'm in another dream.

"I'm afraid," I say in the barest of whispers.

"Of what?"

"The guy she is with now . . . she might . . ."

"So, save him."

FATHER

The day before the day it all ended was a Sunday. The sun was merciless.

All the air conditioners in the house were on full blast, but I could still feel the warmth from outside. Sweat was beading on my forehead. I sat under one of the air conditioners in the upstairs sitting room with no intention of moving. That is, until Ayoola came scrambling up the stairs and found me.

"Dad has a guest!"

We leaned over the balcony to spy on the man. The agbádá he wore kept slipping down his arms, so he was constantly pushing it back up again. It was a rich blue and so large that it was near impossible to tell if there was a slim man or a fat man within the yards of fabric. Ayoola pantomimed pushing her own sleeves back up and we sniggered. We were not afraid of our father when he had guests—he was always on his best behavior. We could laugh and play with little fear of retribution. The guest looked up at us and smiled. His face is forever etched in my mind—it was a square, black, much blacker than I am, with teeth so white he had to have kept his dentist on speed dial. I imagined him getting ṣàkì stuck between his back molars and then immediately demanding to be wheeled in for orthodontic surgery. The thought tickled me and I shared it with Ayoola, who laughed out loud. It caught my father's attention.

"Korede, Ayoola, come and greet my guest."

We trooped down obediently. The guest was already seated, and my mother was offering him delicacy after delicacy. He was important. We knelt down, as was customary, but he waved us back to our feet.

"I am not that old o!" he cried. He and Father laughed even though we could not see what was funny. My feet were hot and itching, and I wanted to go back to the cool of the air conditioner. I switched from foot to foot, hoping my father would dismiss us so that the men could talk business, but Ayoola was transfixed by the visitor's cane. It was studded from top to bottom with different colored beads. Its brightness drew her eye and she went closer to examine it.

The man paused and watched my sister over the rim of his teacup. Seeing her up close, he smiled—but it was not the same smile he had lavished on us earlier.

"Your daughter is very beautiful."

"Really," my father replied, cocking his head.

"Very, very lovely." He moistened his lips. I grabbed Ayoola's hand and pulled her a couple of steps backward. The man looked like a chief, and when we went to the village for Christmas our maternal grandparents always kept us away from chiefs. Apparently, if a chief saw a girl he liked, he would reach out and touch her with his bejeweled cane and she would become his bride, no matter how many wives the man already had; no matter if the girl in question wanted to be his wife or not.

"Hey! What you doing?" Ayoola whined. I hushed her. My father shot me a dark look but said nothing. The way the visitor was eyeing her triggered an instinctive fear inside of me. The visitor's face was moistening with sweat, but even as he wiped his brow with his handkerchief, his eyes did not leave Ayoola's. I waited for Father to put the man in his place. Instead, Father leaned back and stroked the beard that he took great pains to maintain. He looked at Ayoola, as though seeing her for the first time. He was the one man who never referred to Ayoola's stunning features. He treated us both exactly the same. I was never given the impression he was even aware of how gorgeous she was.

Ayoola shifted under his gaze. He rarely looked at us closely, and when he did, it never ended well. She stopped resisting my grip and allowed me to pull her to me. Father redirected his gaze to the chief man. His eyes twinkled.

"Girls, leave us."

We didn't need to be told twice. We ran out of the main living room and shut the door behind us. Ayoola started running up the stairs, but I pressed my ear against the door.

"What are you doing?" she hissed. "If he catches us—"

"Shhhh." I caught words floating through the door, words like "contract," "deal," "girl." The doors were thick oak, so I couldn't hear much else. I joined Ayoola on the stairs and we went to my room.

By the time the sun went down we were out on the balcony, watching the man get into the backseat of his Mercedes and be driven out of our compound. The fear that had been stuck in my throat receded, and I forgot about the incident with the chief man.

FAMILY

Muhtar and I are talking, about the blandness of the food here, the coarseness of the sheets and tall tales of his past students.

There is a knock and Mohammed enters the room, interrupting us. He mumbles a greeting at me, then beams at Muhtar, greeting him in Hausa, to which Muhtar enthusiastically responds. I did not realize they had made each other's acquaintance. And I have never seen Mohammed smile so . . . freely, at someone other than the nurses who fight over him. Their barrage of Hausa relegates me to the position of other and, five minutes in, I decide to leave; but before I have a chance to announce my intentions, there is yet another knock on the door.

One of Muhtar's sons comes in, trailed by a fresh-faced girl. I do not know the names of his children—it hasn't seemed important. But I can tell this is the older one; he is taller and has a full beard. He is thin like his father; they all are, like reeds in the wind. His eyes fall on me. He is probably wondering what a nurse is doing making herself comfortable at his father's bedside, tracing the rim of an empty cup with her finger.

Mohammed empties the wastebasket and shuffles out. I stand up.

"Good morning, Dad."

"Good morning . . . Korede, you are leaving?"

"You have a guest." I nod toward his son.

Muhtar snorts and waves his hand. "Sani, this is Korede, the owner of the voice in my dreams. I'm sure you won't mind her staying."

The son frowns with displeasure. On closer inspection, he does not look as much like his father as I thought. His eyes are small but wide-set, so that he looks permanently surprised. He gives a stiff nod, and I sit back down.

"Dad, this is Miriam, the girl I want to marry," he announces. Miriam lowers herself into a tsugunnawa out of respect for the man she hopes will be her father-in-law.

Muhtar narrows his eyes. "What happened to the last one you brought to meet me?"

His son sighs. It is a long dramatic sigh. "It didn't work out, Dad. You've been out of it for so long . . ." I should have left the room when I had a chance.

"I don't understand what that means. Hadn't I already met her parents?"

Miriam is still kneeling, her right palm cupping her left. The two men seem to have forgotten that she is still here. If this is the first time she is hearing of another woman, it does not seem to register. She glances up at me, her eyes empty. She reminds me of Bunmi. Her face is round, and she is all curves and soft flesh. Her skin is even darker than my own—she comes close to the color black that we are all labeled with. I wonder how old she is.

"I have changed my mind about her, Dad."

"And the money that has been spent?"

"It's just money. Isn't my happiness more important?"

"This is the madness you tried to pull while I was sick?"

"Dad, I want to begin the arrangements, and I need you to—"

"Sani, if you think you are getting a dime from me, you are more foolish than I thought. Miriam, your name is Miriam, abi? Get up. I apologize, but I will not sanction this marriage." Miriam stumbles to her feet and then goes to stand beside Sani.

Sani scowls at me, as though I were somehow to blame for this turn of events. I meet his glare with a look of indifference. A man like him could never ruffle my feathers. But Muhtar catches the exchange.

"Look at me, Sani, not Korede."

"Why is she even here? This is a family matter!"

The truth is, I am asking myself the same question. Why does Muhtar want me here? We both look to him for an answer, but he seems to be in no hurry to provide one.

"I have said all I intend to say on this matter."

▮▮▮

Sani grabs Miriam's hand and spins around, dragging her out of the room with him. Muhtar closes his eyes.

"Why did you want me to remain here?" I ask.

"For your strength," he replies.

SHEEP

After I tire of tossing and turning, I decide to go to Ayoola's room. When we were young, we often slept together, and it always had the effect of calming us both. Together, we were safe.

She is wearing a long cotton tee and hugging a brown teddy bear. Her knees are bent toward her stomach and she does not stir as I slip into bed beside her. This is no surprise. Ayoola wakes up only when her body has tired of sleeping. She does not dream, she does not snore. She lapses into a coma that even the likes of Muhtar cannot fathom.

I envy her for this. My body is exhausted, but my mind is working overtime, remembering and plotting and second-guessing. I am more haunted by her actions than she is. We may have escaped punishment, but our hands are no less bloody. We lie in our bed, in relative comfort even as Femi's body is succumbing to the water and the fish. I am tempted to shake Ayoola awake, but what good would it do? Even if I succeeded in rousing her, she would tell me that it would all be fine and promptly go back to sleep.

Instead I count—sheep, ducks, chickens, cows, goats, bush rats and corpses. I count them to oblivion.

FATHER

Ayoola had a guest. It was the summer holidays, and he had come in the hope of making her his girlfriend before school resumed. I think his name was Ola. I remember he was gangly, with a birthmark that discolored half his face. I remember he could not keep his eyes off Ayoola.

Father received him well. He was offered drinks and snacks. He was coaxed into talking about himself. He was even shown the knife. As far as Ola was concerned, our father was a generous, attentive host. Even Mum and Ayoola had been fooled by the performance—they were both smiling. But I was on the edge of my seat, my fingernails dug into the upholstery.

Ola knew better than to tell the father of the girl he wanted to date that he was interested in her, but you could see it in the way he kept glancing at Ayoola, how he angled his body toward her, how he constantly said her name.

"This boy is a smooth talker o!" Father announced with a chuckle, after Ola had made some well-meaning comment about helping the homeless to find work. "I'm sure you are popular with the ladies."

"Yes, sir. No, sir," he stammered, caught off guard.

"You like my daughters, eh? They are lovely, eh?" Ola blushed. His eyes darted to Ayoola again. Father's jaw clenched. I looked around me, but Ayoola and my mother had not noticed. I remember wishing I had taught Ayoola some type of code. I coughed.

"Pèlé," Mother told me in her soothing voice. I coughed again. "Go and drink water." I coughed once more. Nothing.

Ayoola, follow me, I mouthed, my eyes wide.

"No, thanks."

"Follow me now," I hissed. She crossed her arms and looked back at Ola. She was enjoying his attention too much to mind me. Father turned his head in my direction and smiled. Then I followed his eyes to the cane.

The cane lay ten inches above the TV on a specially crafted ledge. And there it stayed all day, every day. My eyes were constantly drawn to it. To the uninitiated, it must have looked like a work of art—a nod to history and culture. It was thick, smooth and marked with intricate carvings.

The visit passed slowly until Father decided it was over, guiding Ola to the door, telling him to come again and wishing him luck. Then he walked across the silent living room and reached for the cane.

"Ayoola, come here." She looked up, saw the cane and

trembled. Mother trembled. I trembled. "Are you deaf? I said come here!"

"But I did not ask him to come," she whined, instantly understanding what the matter was. "I didn't invite him."

"Please, sir, please," I whispered. I was already crying. "Please."

"Ayoola." She stepped forward. She had started crying too. "Strip."

She removed her dress, button by button. She did not hurry, she fumbled, she cried. But he was patient.

"Nítorí Ọlọrun, Kehinde, please. Nítorí Ọlọrun." Because of God, Mother begged. Because of God. Ayoola's dress fell in a pool at her feet. She was wearing a white training bra and white panties. Even though I was older, I still had no use for a bra. Mother was clinging to Father's shirt, but he brushed her off. She was never able to stop him.

I took a bold step forward and took Ayoola's hand in my own. History had shown me that if you came within reach of the cane, the cane would not distinguish between victim and observer, but I had a feeling Ayoola would not survive the confrontation without me.

"So, I am sending you to school to sleep around, abi?"

You hear the sound of a cane before you feel it. It whips the air. She cried out, and I shut my eyes.

"I am paying all that money for you to be a prostitute?! Answer me na!"

"No, sir." We didn't call him Daddy. We never had. He was not a daddy, at least not in the way the word "daddy" denotes. One could hardly consider him a father. He was the law in our home.

"You think you are all that, abi? I will teach you who is all that!" He struck her again. This time, the cane grazed me, too. I sucked in my breath.

"You think this boy cares about you? He just wants what is between your legs. And when he is done he will move on."

Pain has a way of sharpening your senses. I can still hear his heavy breathing. He was not a fit man. He quickly tired during a beating, but he had a strong will and a stronger desire to instill discipline. I can still remember the smell of our fear—acidic, metallic, sharper even than the smell of vomit.

He continued to give his sermon as he wielded his weapon. Ayoola's skin was light enough that you could see that it was turning red. Because I was not the target, the cane would only occasionally catch me, on my shoulder or ear or the side of my face, but even so, the pain was hard to bear. I could feel Ayoola's grip on my hand weakening. Her cries had turned into a low whimper. I needed to act. "If you beat her any more, she will scar and people will ask questions!"

His hand stilled. If there was one thing in the world he actually cared about, it was his reputation. He seemed momentarily uncertain of what to do next, but then he wiped the sweat off his brow and returned the cane to its resting place. Ayoola sank to the floor beside me.

Not long after, when we were back at school, Ola approached me during break to deliver his thoughts about my father.

"Your dad is really cool," he told me. "I wish my dad was like him."

As for Ayoola, she never spoke to Ola again.

WIFE

"If you don't like these shoes, I have more in storage. I can send you pictures." Bunmi and I look down at the avalanche of shoes that Chichi has poured onto the floor behind the nurses' station. Her shift has been over for at least thirty minutes. She has changed her clothes, and apparently her profession, too—she's gone from nurse to saleswoman. She bends over, shuffling through the shoes on the floor to find the ones we just *have* to buy. She bends over so far that we see her ass crack appear above her jeans. I avert my eyes.

I was minding my own business, scheduling in a patient, when she stuck a pair of black pumps under my nose. I had waved her away, but she insisted that I come and check out her merchandise. The thing is, all the shoes she is selling look cheap, the type that fall apart after a month. She hasn't even bothered to polish them and now they are lying on the floor. I force a smile onto my face.

"You know, they haven't paid salaries yet . . ."

"And I just bought a couple new shoes . . ." Bunmi joins in.

Chichi squares her shoulders and wiggles a pair of diamante heels at us. "You can never have too many shoes. My prices are very reasonable."

She is just about to launch into a sales pitch for a pair of nine-inch wedges when Yinka runs to us and slams her palms down on the counter. She may not be my favorite person in the world, but I am grateful for the interruption.

"There is drama in the coma man's room o!"

"Drama ke?" Chichi forgets her shoes and rests her elbow on my shoulder as she leans forward. I resist the urge to swipe her arm away.

"Eh, I was going to see my patient and I heard shouting coming from his room."

"He was shouting?" I ask her.

"It's the wife who is shouting o. I stopped to . . . make sure he was okay . . . and I heard her calling him the devil. That he cannot take his money to the grave with him."

"Hey! I hate stingy men!" Chichi repeatedly snaps her fingers over her head, warding off any stingy man who might be tempted to come near her. I open my mouth to defend Muhtar, to tell them that he doesn't have a stingy bone in his body, that he is generous and kind—but I look at Bunmi's dull eyes, Chichi's thirsty ones and Yinka's dark pupils and I know that my words would be willfully misinterpreted. Instead, I stand up quickly, and Chichi stumbles.

"Where are you going?"

"We can't allow our patients to be harassed by friends or family. As long as they are here, they are in our care," I call back to her.

"You should put that on a bumper sticker," yells Yinka. I pretend I haven't heard her, and I take the steps two at a time. There are thirty rooms on the third floor: 301 to 330. I hear the shouting as soon as I am in the corridor. There's the nasal voice of the wife, and a man's voice, too. It is whining and cajoling, so I know it is not Muhtar.

I knock on the door, and the voices quiet.

"Come in," Muhtar calls out wearily. I open the door to find him standing by the bed, wearing a gray jalabia. He grips one of the handrails, and I can see he is half leaning on it. The strain on his body shows on his face. He looks older than the last time I saw him.

His wife is draped in a red lace mayafi. It covers her hair and falls over her right shoulder. Her dress is tailored from the same material. Her skin glows, but the snarl on her face is like that of a beast's. Muhtar's brother, Abdul, stands beside her with his eyes cast down. I suppose he is the owner of the whiny voice.

"Yes?" the wife barks at me.

I ignore her. "Muhtar?"

"I'm okay," he reassures me.

"Would you like me to stay?"

"What do you mean, would he like you to stay? You are a common nurse, come on, get out of here!"

Her voice is like nails on a blackboard.

"Did you hear me?" she screeches.

I walk over to Muhtar and he gives me a wan smile.

"I think you should sit down," I tell him gently. He loosens his grip on the bar and I help him settle into the chair closest to him. I lay his blanket over his lap. "Do you want them to stay?" I whisper.

"What is she saying to him?" the wife splutters behind me. "She is a witch! She has used juju to useless my husband! She is the reason why he is not making sense. Abdul, do something. Send her out!" She points at me. "I will report you. I don't know what black magic you are using . . ."

Muhtar shakes his head, and that is all the sign I need. I straighten up and face her.

"Madam, please leave, or I will have to have Security escort you out."

Her lower lip trembles and her eyes twitch. "Who do you think you are talking to? Abdul!"

I turn to Abdul, but he doesn't lift his eyes to meet mine. He is younger than Muhtar, and may be even taller, but it is hard to tell for he has bent his head so low that it threatens to fall off his neck. He rubs her arm in an attempt to soothe her, but she shrugs him off. To be honest, I'd shrug him off too. The suit he is wearing is expensive, but the fit is poor. It is too wide at the shoulders and too broad at the chest. It could easily belong to someone else—the way the woman whose arm he rubs belongs to someone else.

I look at her again. She may have been beautiful once. Maybe the first time Muhtar laid eyes on her.

"I do not mean to be rude," I tell her, "but my patient's well-being is my priority and we don't allow anyone to jeopardize that."

"Who do you think you are?! You think you will get money from him? Abi, has he already given you money? Muhtar, you are there acting all high and mighty, and now you are chasing a nurse. See you! You could not even pick a fine one!"

"Get out!" The order comes from Muhtar and makes us all jump. There is an authority to his voice I have not heard before. Abdul raises his head and quickly lowers it again. The wife glowers at us both before turning on her heel and marching out the door, with Abdul following limply behind. I drag a chair over and sit beside Muhtar. His eyes are heavy. He pats one of my hands. "Thank you."

"It was you who got them out."

He sighs.

"Apparently, Miriam's father wants to run for governor of Kano state."

"So your wife wants you to approve the union."

"Yes."

"And will you?"

"Would you?" I think of Tade, ring in hand, eyes on me, waiting for my blessing.

"Are they in love?"

"Who?"

"Miriam and . . . your son."

"Love. What a novel concept." He closes his eyes.

NIGHT

Tade stares at me, but his eyes are empty. His face is bloated, distorted. He reaches out to touch me and his hands are cold.

"You did this."

BROKEN

I slither inside Tade's office and rummage through his desk drawers to retrieve the ring box. Tade has taken a patient to radiology, so I know I'm alone. The ring is as enchanting as I remember. I am tempted to slip it on my finger. Instead I grip the band tightly, kneel on the floor and strike the diamond against the tiles. I use every ounce of force in my body and strike again. I guess it's true that diamonds are forever—it withstands my every attempt to break it, but the rest of the ring is not as strong willed. Soon the setting is in pieces on the ground. The diamond looks smaller and less impressive without its casing.

It occurs to me that if I just damage the ring, Tade will suspect me. I slip the diamond in my pocket. After all, no self-respecting thief would leave it here. Besides, this would all be a colossal waste of time if Tade simply bought another setting. I head to the medicine cabinet.

Twenty minutes later, Tade storms toward the reception desk. I hold my breath. He looks at me and then quickly looks away, addressing Yinka and Bunmi instead.

"Someone has turned my office upside down and destroyed the . . . some of my things."

"What?!" we cry in unison.

"Are you serious?" adds Yinka, though it is clear from Tade's furrowed brows that something is not right.

We follow him to his office, and he flings open the door. I try to look at it from the eyes of an objective party. It appears as though someone was searching for something and then lost control. The drawers are all open and most of the contents scattered on the floor. The medicine cabinet is ajar, the pill bottles are in disarray and there are files scattered all over his desk. When I left, the broken ring setting was on the ground, but I can no longer see it.

"This is terrible," I mumble.

"Who would do this?" Bunmi asks, frowning.

Yinka purses her lips together and claps her hands. "I saw Mohammed go inside to clean earlier on," she reveals, and I rub my tingling hands on my thighs.

"I don't think Mohammed would—" begins Tade.

"When you left your office, it was normal, yes?" interrupts Yinka.

"Yes."

"Then you went to do the X-ray and the ECG with a patient. How long were you gone?"

"About forty minutes."

"Well, I *saw* Mohammed go into your office in that time. Let's say he spent twenty minutes sweeping the floor and emptying the dustbin. It doesn't give anyone else enough time to enter, do all this and leave," concludes Yinka, the amateur detective.

"Why do you think he would do this?" I ask. She can't hang him without a motive, can she?

"Drugs, obviously," she states. She crosses her arms, satisfied that she has made her case. It's easy to point the finger at Mohammed. He is poor, uneducated. He is a cleaner.

"No." It is Bunmi who speaks, Bunmi who protests. "I don't accept that." She is eyeing Yinka, and because I am beside Yinka she is eyeing me too. Or does she suspect something? "This man has been working in this place for longer than the both of you and there has never been a problem. He wouldn't do this." I have never seen Bunmi speak so passionately, or for so long. We all stare at her.

"Drug addicts can hide their addiction for a long time," argues Yinka finally. "He was probably suffering from withdrawal or something. When these people need a hit . . . Who knows how long he has been stealing drugs and getting away with it."

Yinka is content with her conclusion, and Tade is deep in thought. Bunmi walks away. I have done the right thing . . . right? I have bought Tade more time to think things through. I want to volunteer to clean up, but I know I should keep my distance.

Mohammed denies the charges vehemently, but he is fired anyway. I can see the decision does not sit well with Tade, but the evidence, or lack of evidence, is not in Mohammed's favor. It worries me that Tade does not mention the broken ring to me. In fact, he has not sought me out at all.

"Hey," I say a few days later, standing in the doorway of his office.

"What's up?" He does not look at me, but continues writing in his file.

"I . . . I just wanted to check that everything is alright with you."

"Yeah, everything is cool."

"I didn't want to ask in front of the others . . . but I hope the ring wasn't stolen . . ."

He stops writing and puts his pen down. He looks at me for the first time. "Actually, Korede, it was."

I'm about to feign shock and commiserate, when he continues.

"But what is funny is that the two bottles of diazepam in the cabinet weren't. The drugs were all over the place, but the ring was the *only* thing that was actually taken. Curious behavior, for a drug addict."

He holds my gaze. I refuse to blink or look away. I can feel my eyeballs drying out. "Very curious," I manage.

We stare at each other for a while longer, then he sighs and rubs his face. "Okay," he says, almost to himself. "Okay. Is there anything else?"

"No . . . no. Not at all."

That night I drop the diamond into the third mainland bridge lagoon.

PHONE

I have found that the best way to take your mind off something is to binge-watch TV shows. The hours pass by and I lie on my bed, stuffing my mouth with groundnuts and staring at my laptop screen. I lean forward and type in the address to Femi's blog, but my efforts are met with a 404. His blog has been taken down. He no longer exists for the online world; he can no longer exist for me. He is beyond my reach now in death, as he would have been in life.

My phone vibrates and I consider ignoring it, but I reach forward and drag it toward me.

It's Ayoola.

My heart skips a beat.

"Hello?"

"Korede."

#2: PETER

"Korede, he's dead."

"What?"

"He's . . ."

"What the hell? What are you saying? He's . . . you . . . you . . ?"

She burst into tears.

"Please. Please. Help me."

THEATER

This is the first time I will be entering Tade's home. I imagined this moment in several different ways, but never like this. I bang on the door and then I bang again, not caring who hears or sees as long as the door is opened in time.

I hear the click of the door and step back. Tade stands there, sweat rolling off his face and neck, in spite of the blast of air conditioning that hits me. I push past him and look around. I see his living room, his kitchen, stairs. I don't see Ayoola.

"Where is she?"

"Upstairs," he whispers. I run up the stairs, calling out to Ayoola, but she does not reply. She can't be dead. She can't be. Life without her . . . And if she is gone, it is my fault for saying more than I should have. I *knew* that this could only ever be the case—to save him, I've sacrificed her.

"Turn left," he says from close behind me. I open the door. My hand is shaking. I am in his bedroom—the king-sized bed takes up a third of the room, and on the other side of it I hear a low moan.

For a moment I am too scared to react. She is slumped on the floor, much the same way that Femi was, pressing her hand to her side. I can see the blood spilling through her fingers, but the knife—her knife—is still in her. She looks at me and gives me a weak smile.

"The irony," she says. I rush to her side.

"She . . . she . . . tried to kill me."

I ignore him and use the scissors in my first aid kit to cut off the bottom half of my shirt, after the bandages prove too paltry to do the job. I wanted to call an ambulance, but I couldn't risk Tade talking to anyone till I got to her.

"I didn't take out the knife," she tells me.

"Good girl."

I use my jacket as a pillow and help her lie down. She moans again and it feels as though someone were squeezing my heart. I take medical gloves out of the kit and slip them on.

"I didn't mean to hurt her."

"Ayoola, tell me what happened." I don't really want to know what happened, but I need her to keep talking.

"He . . . he . . . hit me—" she begins as I cut her dress open.

"I did not hit her!" cries Tade—the first man able to defend himself against Ayoola's accusations.

". . . then I tried to stop him and he stabbed me."

"She came at me with a knife! Out of nowhere! Shit!"

"Shut up!" I tell him. "You're not the one lying here bleeding out, are you?"

I bandage her wound with the knife still in it. If I took it out, I'd risk nicking an artery or organ. I grab my phone and call the reception desk at the hospital. Chichi picks up, and I silently thank God that Yinka's not on night shifts this week. I explain to her that I'll be coming with my sister who has been stabbed and I ask her to call in Dr. Akigbe.

"I'll carry her," Tade says. I don't want him touching her, but he is stronger than I am.

"Fine."

He scoops her up and brings her down the stairs and out onto the drive. She rests her head against his chest as though they were somehow still lovers. Perhaps she cannot yet understand the gravity of what has taken place here.

I open the rear door of my car and he lays her in the back. I jump in the driver's seat. He tells me he will follow us in his car, and since I can't do anything to stop him, I nod. It's 4 a.m., so traffic is sparse and there are no police officers in sight. I take full advantage of this, driving 130 kilometers an hour on one-way roads. We get to the hospital in twenty minutes.

Chichi and a trauma team meet us at the entrance. "What happened?" Chichi asks, while two porters slide my little sister out onto a gurney. She's no longer conscious.

"What *happened*?" she insists.

"She got stabbed."

"By who?"

Dr. Akigbe materializes as we are halfway through the corridor. He checks Ayoola's pulse and then barks orders at the nurses. As my sister is wheeled away, he ushers me into a side room.

"Can't I go in with her?"

"Korede, you're going to have to wait outside."

"But—"

"You know the rules. And you've done all you can do for the moment. You requested me, so trust me."

He sweeps out of the room and into the surgical theater. I walk into the hallway just as Tade runs up, breathless.

"Is she in theater?"

I don't respond. He reaches out to touch me. "Don't." He drops his hand.

"You know I didn't mean to do it, right? We were both struggling with it and I . . ." I turn my back on him and head to the water dispenser. He follows me. "You said yourself that she's dangerous." I'm quiet. There isn't anything to say anymore. "Did you tell anyone what happened?" he asks in a quiet voice.

"No," I say, pouring a cup of water. I'm surprised at how steady my hand is. "And you're not going to either."

"What?"

"If you say anything about any of this, I will tell them that you attacked her. And who do you think they will believe. You or Ayoola?"

"You *know* I'm innocent. You know I was defending myself."

"I know I walked in and my sister had a knife in her side. That's all I know."

"She tried to kill me! You can't . . ." He blinks at me, as though seeing me for the first time. "You're worse than she is."

"Excuse me?"

"There's something wrong with her . . . but you? What's your excuse?" He walks away from me then in disgust.

I sit in the corridor outside the operating theater and wait for news.

WOUND

Dr. Akigbe comes out of the room and smiles at me. I breathe out.

"Can I see her?"

"She is sleeping. We are going to take her to a room upstairs. Once she is settled, you can pop in."

They put Ayoola in room 315, two doors away from Muhtar, who has never seen my sister but knows more about her than I ever intended.

She looks innocent, vulnerable. Her chest rises and falls gently. Someone has laid her dreads carefully beside her on the bed.

"Who did this to her?" It is Yinka. She looks upset.

"I'm just glad she is okay."

"Whoever did this should be killed!" Her face has contorted into a mixture of fury and contempt. "If it wasn't for you, she probably would have died!"

"I . . . I . . ."

"Ayoola!" My mum rushes in, her heart in her mouth. "My baby!" She leans over the bed and lowers her cheek to her unconscious daughter's mouth—to feel her breath, like she used to do sometimes when Ayoola was still a baby. When she straightens, she is crying. She stumbles into me, and I put my arms around her. Yinka excuses herself.

"Korede, what happened? Who did this?"

"She called me. I came to get her from where she was. She had the knife in her."

"Where did you pick her up from?"

Ayoola moans and we both turn to look at her, but she is still sleeping and she quickly settles back into the task of breathing in and out.

"I'm sure Ayoola will be able to tell us both what took place when she gets up."

"But where did you find her? Why won't you tell me?"

I wonder what Tade is doing, what he is thinking and what his next move will be. I will Ayoola to wake, so that we can agree on whatever story needs to be told. Anything but the truth.

"She was at Tade's house . . . I believe he found her there, like that."

"Tade? Was there a break-in? Could . . . could *Tade* have done it?"

"I don't know, Mum." I suddenly feel exhausted. "We'll ask Ayoola when she wakes." Mum frowns, but says nothing. All we can do now is wait.

FENCE

The hospital room is tidy, mostly because I have been setting it to rights for the past thirty minutes. The teddy bears I brought from home are arranged at the foot of the bed, according to color—yellow, brown, black. Ayoola's phone is fully charged, so the charger has been wrapped around itself and placed in her bag—which I took the liberty of also rearranging. Her bag was a mess—used tissue, receipts, cookie crumbs, notes from Dubai and candy that had been sucked and rewrapped. I take a pen and write down the things I have thrown away, in case she asks.

"Korede?"

I pause what I'm doing and look at Ayoola, whose big bright eyes are looking at me.

"Hey . . . you're awake. How do you feel?"

"Like hell."

I stand up and fetch her a cup of water. I hold it to her lips and she drinks.

"Better?"

"A little . . . where's Mum?"

"She went home to have a shower. She should be back soon."

Ayoola nods, and then closes her eyes. She is asleep again within the minute.

The next time Ayoola wakes, she is more alert. She looks around, taking in her surroundings. I don't believe she has ever been in a hospital room before. She never has anything worse than the common cold, and everyone close to her has died before they reached the hospital.

"It's so boring . . ."

"Would you like someone to paint graffiti on the walls for you, o great one?"

"No, not graffiti . . . *art*." I laugh, and she laughs with me. There is a knock on the door, but before we say a word, the door opens.

It's the police. A different pair from the ones who questioned us about Femi. One of them is a woman. They make a beeline for Ayoola, and I block them.

"Excuse me, can I help you?"

"We understand that she was stabbed."

"Yes?"

"We just want to ask a few questions, find out who it was," replies the woman, looking over my shoulder while I try to hustle them out.

"It was Tade," says Ayoola. Just like that. *It was Tade.* She doesn't pause or hesitate. They could have asked her what the weather was and she wouldn't have sounded more relaxed. The floor is unsteady beneath me and I grab onto a chair and sit down.

"And who is this Tade?"

"He is a doctor here," my mum adds, materializing as though from thin air. She looks at me strangely, probably trying to understand why I look like I am about to throw up. I should have talked to Ayoola as soon as she woke up the first time.

"Can you tell us what happened?"

"He proposed to me and I said I wasn't interested and he lost it. He attacked me."

"How did your sister get to you?"

"He left the room and I called her." They glance at me, but they don't ask me any questions, which is good because I doubt that I would be very coherent.

"Thank you, ma'am. We'll be back."

They run out, no doubt to locate Tade.

"Ayoola, what are you doing?"

"What do you mean what is she doing? That man stabbed your sister!"

Ayoola nods fervently, as outraged as our mother.

"Ayoola, listen to me. You will ruin that man's life."

"It's him or me, Korede."

"Ayoola . . ."

"You can't sit on the fence forever."

SCREEN

The next time I see Muhtar's wife, she is leaning against the wall of the corridor. Her shoulders are trembling, but no sound escapes her lips. Did no one tell her it is painful to cry silently?

She senses she is not alone; her shoulders still and she looks up. Her eyes narrow and her lips twist into a sneer, but she does not wipe the snot that is trailing from her nose to her lip. I find myself taking a few steps backward. Grief can be contagious and I have enough problems of my own.

She hitches up her dress and pushes past me in a flurry of lace and a fog of Jimmy Choo L'Eau. She's careful to catch me with the sharp point of her bony shoulder. I wonder where her brother-in-law is and why he is not by her side. I try not to breathe in the pungent smell of perfume and sadness as I head into room 313.

Muhtar is seated on his bed, with the remote control pointed at the TV. He puts it down when he sees me and flashes me a warm smile, though his eyes are tired.

"I saw your wife on the way here."

"Oh?"

"She was crying."

"Oh."

I wait for him to add something more, but he chooses to pick up the remote control and continue flicking through channels. He does not seem surprised or disturbed by what I've told him. Or particularly interested. I may as well have told him that I saw a wall gecko on the way to work.

"Did you ever love her?"

"Once upon a time . . ."

"Perhaps she still loves you."

"She does not cry for me," he says, his voice hardening. "She cries for her lost youth, her missed opportunities and her limited options. She does not cry for me, she cries for herself."

He settles on a channel—NTA. It's like watching television from the nineties—the reporter has a green-gray tint and the transmission flickers and jumps. We both stare at the screen, at the danfo buses zooming past and the passersby craning their necks to take a look at what is being filmed. He's muted the sound, so I have no idea what is happening.

"I heard about what happened to your sister."

"News travels fast around here."

"I'm sorry."

I smile at him. "I suppose it was only a matter of time."

"She tried to hurt someone again."

I don't say anything—but then he didn't phrase it as a question. On the TV, the woman has now stopped to interview a passerby and his eyes continually flit between her and the camera, as though he is unsure whom he should be making his case to.

"You can do it, you know."

"Do what?"

"Free yourself. Tell the truth."

I can feel his gaze on me now. The TV has started to blur. I blink, blink again and swallow. No words come out. The truth. The truth is that my sister was hurt on my watch because of something I said, and I regret it.

He senses my discomfort and changes the subject. "They are discharging me tomorrow."

I turn to meet his eyes. He wasn't going to be here forever. He isn't a chair or a bed or a stethoscope; he is a patient, and patients leave—alive or dead. And yet, I feel something akin to surprise, akin to fear.

"Oh?"

"I do not want to lose touch," he tells me.

It is funny, the only times I ever touched Muhtar was when he was sleeping or at the gate between life and death, when it was necessary to move his body for him. Now he turns his head back to face the screen on his own.

"Maybe you can give me your number and I can WhatsApp you?"

I cannot think of what to say. Does Muhtar exist outside these walls? Who is he? Besides a man who knows my deepest secrets. And Ayoola's. He has a strangely European nose, this keeper of confidences. It is sharp and long. I wonder what his own secrets are. But then I do not even know what his hobbies are, what his shackles are, where he rested his head at night before he was carried into the hospital on a stretcher.

"Or I can give you my number and you can call anytime you need to talk."

I nod. I am not sure he sees the nod. His eyes are still fixed to the screen. I decide to leave. When I get to the door, I turn around. "Perhaps your wife still loves you."

He sighs. "You cannot take back words, once they've been spoken."

"What words?"

"I divorce you. I divorce you. I divorce you."

SISTER

Ayoola is lying on her bed, angling her body to show Snapchat her injury. I wait for her to finish, and she eventually pulls her shirt back down over her stitches, puts her phone to one side and grins at me. Even now, she looks blameless. She is wearing cotton shorts and a white camisole and is holding on to one of the plush bears on her bed.

"Will you tell me what happened?"

On the bedside table is an open box of candy, a get-well-soon gift. She plucks out a lollipop, unwraps it and sticks it in her mouth, sucking on it thoughtfully.

"Between Tade and me?"

"Yeah."

She sucks some more.

"He said you broke my ring. Said you were accusing me of all sorts and that maybe you had something to do with my ex going missing . . ."

"What . . . what . . . did you say?"

"I told him he was crazy. But he said you were really jealous of me and had some kind of . . . umm . . . latent anger . . . that what if"—she pauses for dramatic effect—

"what if you had gone back, after we left, you know, to talk to Femi . . ."

"He thinks I killed Femi?!" I grab Ayoola's arm, even though she is not to blame this time. How could he think I was capable of that?

"Weird, right? I didn't even tell him about Femi. Only Gboye. Maybe he saw it on Insta. Anyway, it's like he wanted to report you or something . . . So I did what I had to do." She shrugs. "Or at least I tried."

She grabs a bear, buries her head in it and is quiet.

"And then?"

"Then when I was on the ground, he was all like, oh my gooooosh, Korede was telling the truth. What *did* you tell him, Ko-re-de?"

She did this for me and ended up hurt because I betrayed her. I feel dizzy. I don't want to admit that I chose a man's welfare over hers. I don't want to confess to letting him come between us, when she clearly chose me over him. "I . . . I told him you were dangerous."

She sighs and asks, "What do you think will happen now?"

"There will be an investigation of sorts."

"Will they believe his story?

"I don't know . . . it's his word against yours."

"Against ours, Korede. It's his word against *ours*."

FATHER

Yoruba people have a custom of naming twins Taiwo and Kehinde. Taiwo is the older twin, the one who comes out first. Kehinde, therefore, is the second-born twin. But Kehinde is also the older twin, because he says to Taiwo, "Go out first and test the world for me."

This is certainly how Father considered his position as the second twin. And Aunty Taiwo agreed—she did everything he told her to and held an unquestioning trust in everything he did. Which is how—doing what she was told, unquestioningly—she found herself in the house with us the Monday before our father died, shouting at me to let go of Ayoola.

"No!" I screamed, pulling Ayoola even closer to me. My father was not around and, though I knew I would pay for my obstinacy later, later was a while away. His absence now gave me courage, and the promise of his return made me determined.

"Your father will hear of this," Aunty Taiwo threatened. But I couldn't have cared less. I had already begun to develop plans in my head for Ayoola's and my escape.

Ayoola held on to me tighter, even as I promised I would not let her go.

"Please," Mother moaned from one of the corners in the room. "She is too young."

"She should not have been flirting with her father's guest, then."

My mouth dropped open in disbelief. What lies had my father been telling? And why did he insist that Ayoola go to meet the chief man in his home, alone? I must have uttered the question out loud because Aunty Taiwo replied, "She will not be alone; I will be there." As though that were any kind of reassurance. "Ayoola, it is important that you do this for your father," she said in a wheedling voice. "This business opportunity is very critical. He will buy you whatever phone you want, when he gets the contract. Isn't that exciting?!"

"Don't make me go," Ayoola cried.

"You are not going anywhere," I told her.

"Ayoola," Aunty Taiwo coaxed, "you are not a child anymore. You have started menstruating. Many girls would be excited about this. This man will give you anything you want. Anything."

"Anything?" Ayoola asked between sniffs. I slapped her to bring her back to her senses. But I understood. Half of her fear was because I was afraid. She did not really know what they were demanding from her. Granted, she was fourteen, but fourteen then was younger than fourteen now.

This was my father's last gift to us. This arrangement he had made with another man. But he had also passed on his strength to me, and I decided he was not getting his way, not this time. Ayoola was my responsibility and mine alone.

I grabbed the cane from its pedestal and waved it before me. "Aunty, if you come near us, I will beat you with this cane and I will not stop until he comes home."

She was about to call my bluff. She was taller than I, heavier than I—but she looked into my eyes and took a few steps backward. Emboldened, I took a swipe at her. She retreated farther. I let go of Ayoola and chased Aunty Taiwo out of the house, brandishing the cane. When I returned, Ayoola was shaking.

"He will kill us," she sobbed.

"Not if we kill him first."

TRUTH

"Dr. Otumu states that he acted in self-defense and that you can verify this. He says, and I quote: 'She warned me that Ayoola had killed before.' Ms. Abebe, has your sister killed before?"

"No."

"What did you mean when you told him that your sister had killed before?" My interviewers are well spoken and well educated. But this comes as no real surprise. Tade is a talented doctor at a prestigious hospital, Ayoola a beautiful woman from a "good" background. The case screams "high profile." My hands are resting one atop the other on my lap. I would have preferred to place them on the table, but the table is grimy. There is a faint smile on my lips because I am humoring them and they should know that I am humoring them—but it is not enough of a smile to suggest that I find the circumstances at all humorous. My mind is clear.

"A man died of food poisoning on a trip with my sister. I was angry that she went with him, because he was married. I believed their actions led to his death."

"What of her ex-boyfriend?"

"Tade?"

"Femi; the one who went missing."

I lean forward; my eyes light up. "Has he come back? Has he said something?"

"No."

I frown, lean back and lower my eyes. If I could, I would squeeze out a tear, but I have never been able to cry on cue.

"So why do you think she has anything to do with that?"

"We suspect that—"

"A hundred suspicions don't make proof. She is five-two. What the hell do you think she did with him, if she hurt him?" My lips are firm, my eyes disbelieving. I shake my head slightly for good measure.

"So you believe she may have hurt him?"

"No. My sister is the sweetest person you'll ever meet. Have you met her?" They shift uncomfortably. They have met her. They have looked into her eyes and fantasized about her. They are all the same.

"What do you think happened that day?"

"All I know is that he stabbed her, and that she was unarmed."

"He said she brought the knife with her."

"Why would she do that? How could she know he would attack her?"

"The knife is missing. Nurse Chichi states that she logged it in after it was removed during surgery. You would have known where it was kept."

"All the nurses know . . . and all the doctors."

"How long have you known Dr. Otumu?"

"Not very long."

"Have you known him to be violent?" When I was picking my outfit, I chose a light gray skirt suit. It is solemn, feminine, and a subtle reminder that the police and I are not from the same social class.

"No."

"So you admit that this is out of character for him . . ."

"I believe I just said I've not known him very long."

GONE

Muhtar has gone home to begin his life anew. Room 313 is empty. I sit there anyway, in the spot I usually sat when Muhtar was still in the realm between life and death. I picture him on the bed and I feel an intense sense of loss, more so than the one I feel for Tade, who is also gone.

They had his license revoked, and he has to spend a few months in jail for assault. It could have been much worse, but many attested to the fact that he was kind and had never displayed a whit of violence. Still, there was no denying the fact that he stabbed Ayoola. And for that, society demanded that he pay.

I haven't seen him since the day it happened. He was placed on suspension as soon as she accused him, so I don't know what he is thinking or feeling. But I don't much care. She was right. You have to choose a side, and my lot was cast long ago. She will always have me and I will always have her; no one else matters.

Muhtar gave me his number. He wrote it on a piece of paper that I put in the pocket of my uniform.

I still toy with the idea of telling Ayoola that there is

someone out there, free and unconstrained, who knows her secret. That at any point, the things we've done could become public record. But I don't think I will.

The linen used for Muhtar's bed has not been changed. I can tell. I can still smell him in the room— that freshly showered smell he sported in those days of consciousness. I close my eyes for a bit, and allow my mind to wander.

A short while later, I pick up the room phone and dial the number for the fourth floor.

"Please call Mohammed down here, room 313."

"Mohammed is gone, ma."

"Oh . . . yes, of course. Send Assibi."

#5

0809 743 5555

I have keyed in his number three times and I have cleared the screen three times. The paper where his number is written is not as smooth as it once was.

But I am already beginning to forget what his voice sounds like.

There is a knock on my door.

"Come in."

The house girl opens the door a crack and sticks her head in. "Ma, Mummy says I should call you. There is a guest downstairs."

"Who is it?"

"It's a man."

I dismiss her, realizing she can't tell me more than that.

She closes my door and I stare at the slip of paper with Muhtar's number on it. I light a candle on my nightstand and hold the paper over the flame until the numbers are swallowed by blackness and fire licks the tips of my fingers. There will never be another Muhtar, I know this. There will never be another opportunity to

꒐꒐꒐

confess my sins or another chance to absolve myself of the crimes of the past . . . or the future. They disappear with the curling paper, because Ayoola needs me; she needs me more than I need untainted hands.

When I'm done, I walk to the mirror. I am not exactly dressed to entertain guests—I'm wearing a bubu and a turban—but whoever it is will have to take me as I am.

I take the back stairs, pause before the painting. I glimpse the evanescent shadow of the woman, and for a moment it feels as though she watches me from a vantage point that I cannot see. The frame is tilting a little to the left; I correct it and move on. Our house girl scurries by me carrying a vase of roses—the go-to of the unimaginative; but I guess Ayoola will be pleased.

They are in the living room—my mum, Ayoola and the man. All three of them look up at me as I approach.

"This is my sister, Korede."

The man smiles. I smile back.

ACKNOWLEDGMENTS

I am grateful first to God.

To Clare Alexander, thank you, because without you, and the insight you possess, I would still be chugging away in the corner of my room waiting for "the novel" to come along. You are my fairy agentmother. Thank you to everyone at Aitken Alexander, for your efforts and your attention. I am truly appreciative.

To Margo Shickmanter, my U.S. editor, and James Roxburgh, my U.K. editor, thank you for your patience, your warmth and your understanding. Thank you for believing in this book and in me. Thank you for encouraging me to stretch myself; I think the book is far better for it.

Every day I learn how much work goes into publishing a novel, and so I would like to thank the Doubleday team and the Atlantic team for the time spent and the efforts made.

Emeka Agbakuru, Adebola Rayo, thank you for reading, and reading, and reading again. It's a blessing to be able to call you friend.

Obafunke Braithwaite, you are a pain, but without

you, becoming a published author would have been a little overwhelming.

Thank you to Ayobami Adebayo for taking the time to add the accents to my Yoruba. One day, I shall be as fluent as a Lagos goat.